2-13

HOW  tía Lola

JULIA ALVAREZ

Learned to Teach

HOW **tía Lola**

JULIA ALVAREZ

Learned to Teach

ALFRED A. KNOPF
NEW YORK

THIS IS A BORZOI BOOK PUBLISHED BY ALFRED A. KNOPF

Visit us on the Web! www.randomhouse.com/kids

Educators and librarians, for a variety of teaching tools, visit us at
www.randomhouse.com/teachers

Library of Congress Cataloging-in-Publication Data
Alvarez, Julia.
How Tia Lola learned to teach / by Julia Alvarez.—1st ed.
p. cm.
Summary: Juanita and Miguel's great-aunt, Tía Lola, comes from the Dominican Republic to
help take care of them after their parents divorce, and soon she is so involved in their small
Vermont community that when her visa expires, the whole town turns out to support her.
ISBN 978-0-375-86460-5 (trade) — ISBN 978-0-375-96460-2 (lib. bdg.) —
ISBN 978-0-375-89584-5 (e-book) — ISBN 978-0-375-85792-8 (pbk.)
[1. Great-aunts—Fiction. 2. Dominican Americans—Fiction. 3. Family life—Vermont—
Fiction. 4. Community life—Vermont—Fiction. 5. Schools—Fiction. 6. Divorce—Fiction.
7. Vermont—Fiction.] I. Title.
PZ7.A48How 2010
[Fic]—dc22
2010004964

The text of this book is set in 13-point Bembo.

Printed in the United States of America
October 2010
10 9 8 7 6 5 4 3 2

First Edition

for

Tía Rosa,

beloved aunt, second mother,

alive in our hearts forever

1928 2008

contents

before we begin

Coser y cantar, todo es empezar
Sewing and singing, beginning is everything

In the middle of winter in Vermont, Tía Lola feels lonely out in the country all by herself all day long.

In the early morning, she is happy, waking up Miguel and Juanita, getting them ready for school. She races down the driveway to the waiting bus and waves goodbye to them, and later to their mother as she leaves for work.

"¡Adiós! ¡Adiós! ¡Adiós!" Tía Lola calls out. Her breath fades in the cold air. The snowy fields stretch all around her. She closes the door to the big, cold, empty house.

Suddenly, she can hear her heart beating, the refrigerator humming, the radiator clanking, a little bird pecking seeds from the feeder hanging out the window. She turns on the television for company. But Tía Lola doesn't know much English, so she can't understand what all those little people inside the box are saying.

When the phone rings at noon, Tía Lola snatches it up after one ring. Mami is calling to check on how Tía Lola is doing.

"*¡Bien! ¡Bien!*" Tía Lola says, pumping up her voice as if it were a flat tire. She is just fine. She does not want Mami to worry. Or for Miguel and Juanita to think their aunt from the Dominican Republic isn't happy to be staying on in Vermont to take care of them.

But Tía Lola needs something to do.

That is why when the phone rings one cold January night with a surprising request from the school principal, Tía Lola says, "*¡Sí, sí, sí!*" before she even knows what exactly she is agreeing to do.

"She says yes," Mami translates. "She'd love to come to school every day with Juanita and Miguel."

"She's going to do what?!" Miguel can't believe his *mami* would accept Mrs. Stevens's request without first checking with him and his little sister, Juanita. Now he *will* be the laughingstock of Bridgeport Elementary. This time it won't be because his last name, Guzmán, sounds like "Gooseman," or because he looks different from everyone in his class. It'll be because he has brought his own personal, wacky, babysitting aunt who doesn't speak English to school. "But what's Tía Lola going to do there all day?"

"*Coser y cantar, todo es empezar.*" Tía Lola chants one of

2

her sayings: Sewing and singing, beginning is everything. No matter what you do, you just have to jump right in! "I'll go every day and clean the rooms or cook or paint the building a nice bright color," she offers in Spanish.

Mami shakes her head at each of these suggestions. "No, no, no, Tía Lola. What Señora Stevens wants you to do is teach the children some Spanish."

Tía Lola's mouth drops open, but no words, Spanish or English, come out of it.

"It turns out there are several new Spanish speakers at Bridgeport," Mami goes on explaining, "besides you two." She nods at Juanita and Miguel. "Mrs. Stevens said they're from Mexico."

"One of them's in my class," Juanita speaks up. "Her name's Ofelia, but everyone calls her Ofie." Actually, Ofie is in second grade and Juanita is in third, but this year at Bridgeport, second and third graders, as well as fourth and fifth graders, have combined classes. Something to do with how few kids are enrolled in these classes and how much money the principal has to hire new teachers.

"It's such a great opportunity for all the children to learn some Spanish," Mami is saying. "But *la señora* Stevens doesn't have funding to hire a teacher. That's why she hopes you'll volunteer, Tía Lola. Just go and teach the kids some words, and dances, and songs, and tell a few stories. . . ." Mami is trying hard to make it sound easy and fun. But the panic on Tía Lola's face makes even Miguel want to persuade her not to worry.

"¿Qué pasa, Tía Lola?" Juanita cocks her head as if from a different angle she'll be able to tell what's wrong with her aunt. Tía Lola has been saying she wants something to do during the long days in the United States of America. So why isn't she happy about this wonderful news?

"I can't be a teacher." Tía Lola looks the most alarmed any of them have ever seen her.

"¿Por qué?" "Why not?" *"Por qué* not?" They all ask her at the same time, Mami in Spanish, Miguel in English, Juanita in Spanglish.

"Porque . . ." Because . . . Tía Lola bows her head and cannot continue.

"Remember what you yourself said, Tía Lola," Mami says gently. "Sewing and singing, and even teaching—"

"Todo es empezar," Tía Lola mutters, like she doesn't believe it anymore.

"The only way to learn is by starting," Mami adds, throwing another log in the fire. "Look at us. A year ago, when we moved here, who would've thought this drafty old farmhouse would become our warm, cozy home? A few weeks later, when you came to visit, Tía Lola, none of us ever thought you'd stay on to live with us. All these changes began without any of us knowing anything about how to make the next move. And here we are!" Mami smiles enthusiastically.

The fire crackles happily. Outside, a soft snow is falling. Soon the world will be as blank and white as a clean sheet of paper right before you begin to write.

4

lesson one

Buenas razones cautivan los corazones
Good intentions win hearts

"Mami, why is Tía Lola so scared to be a teacher?" Juanita wants to know. Mami is tucking her into bed. Juanita has been pleading for five more minutes so she can read another chapter in her book. But Mami has ruled that Monday through Thursday, lights must be out promptly by eight p.m. Otherwise, Juanita is too tired to pay attention the next day in class.

Mami sighs. "I think Tía Lola doesn't feel confident because she never went past fourth grade."

"I haven't gone past fourth grade either," Juanita reminds her.

"I know, Juanita." Mami smiles fondly at her daughter. "But you're only eight. And Tía Lola, well, she's past fifty. She thinks she's not smart enough to teach the kids at your school."

"But that's ridiculous, Mami!" Juanita says importantly. It feels so grown-up to be able to pronounce something ridiculous. "Tía Lola knows so much. All these stories and songs and sayings. And she knows how to cook and make friends and . . ." Juanita runs out of breath before she has run out of things Tía Lola knows how to do.

"Would you do me a favor, Nita *bonita*?" Her *mami* always calls Juanita by her nickname and then adds the Spanish word for "pretty" when she is asking for something that will take extra effort. "Could you tell your *tía* Lola what you just told me? Tell her you'd love for her to come to your school. That it'll be just like taking care of you and Miguel, except that you'll have a few friends along. . . ."

"Like seventy-four—sorry, seventy-six, counting Nita and me." Miguel is at the door. He must have overheard Mami discussing Mrs. Stevens's invitation.

Mami looks at Miguel in that careful way, trying to figure out what he is feeling. She works at the college, counseling students who feel confused or troubled. Except Miguel isn't confused or troubled. He just thinks that adults should go to work somewhere besides where their kids go to school.

"Do you *not* want Tía Lola to volunteer at Bridgeport?" Mami asks carefully.

Miguel squirms. He's not sure he wants Tía Lola at his school every single day. But his mother is looking disappointed. "How about if Tía Lola just comes sometimes?" Miguel suggests.

"You know, Miguel Ángel Guzmán, you might just have hit on a brilliant idea!"

Miguel blinks in disbelief. "I have?"

"He has?" Juanita echoes.

Mami nods, ignoring the sparks flying between brother and sister. "I think it'll be less scary for Tía Lola to start by volunteering once a week, say. She can think of it as just visiting, not teaching. Then, once she gets used to it, she can go more often."

Like in a year and a half, when I'll already be at the middle school, Miguel thinks. But he knows better than to say so. He doesn't want to upset Mami, who can still be supersensitive. A year ago, at Christmas, his parents separated. His father, Papi, stayed behind in New York City, but Mami moved to Vermont with a job at the college, bringing Miguel and Juanita with her. That's why their aunt came from the Dominican Republic to help take care of them. Miguel has to admit that ever since Tía Lola arrived, Mami is a lot happier. It's Tía Lola who seems sadder.

"Can she start tomorrow?" Juanita pipes up, her eyes bright and hopeful.

"I don't see why not. But I'll need you guys to help me convince her, okay?"

Juanita nods eagerly. Miguel nods as well. After all, it was *his* brilliant idea. . . .

Juanita gets up early the next morning. She doesn't even bother to gaze out her window at the back pasture covered with fresh snow. Instead, she hurries downstairs, hoping to talk Tía Lola into coming to school today.

In the kitchen she finds her aunt frying up some plantains and bacon. *"Buenos días,"* Tía Lola sings out cheerfully. "What are you doing up this early?"

"Oh . . . I just . . . I wanted to . . ." For some reason, Juanita finds it hard to explain. Partly, it's having to talk in Spanish. Only when Miguel is around does Juanita's Spanish seem to really improve.

Tía Lola winks at her niece. *"No por mucho madrugar amanece más temprano."*

This is one of Tía Lola's favorite sayings. Something about how waking up early won't make the sun rise any faster. Tía Lola always quotes this saying when anyone is being too eager a beaver.

"As soon as I'm done with this, I'll help you get ready," Tía Lola offers, turning back to her cooking. Usually, she braids Juanita's hair or finds a missing sock or irons a favorite outfit her niece wants to wear.

It's now or never, Juanita thinks, taking a deep breath. "Tía Lola, aren't *you* going to get ready?" Her aunt is dressed in a colorful robe with parrots and bright flowers and a rainbow draped over her right shoulder. She looks like she does every morning, not like someone who is going to be the volunteer Spanish teacher at school today.

"*¿Preparada para qué?*" Tía Lola asks. Ready for what?

"To go to school with us today."

Tía Lola is shaking her head before Juanita is even done talking. "*Tal vez* maybe another day."

"She won't come with us," Juanita says to Miguel, who has just stepped into the room. "Maybe if you ask her?"

Miguel wasn't planning on carrying out his brilliant idea just yet. But having his little sister admit that he can do something she can't makes him want to try.

"Tía Lola, do you know what day it is today?"

Tía Lola scrunches up her face. So does Juanita. Mami has just walked in from brushing the snow off her car. "Today? What's today?"

"Today is . . ." Miguel has to think fast. He flashes an SOS look at Juanita. *Help me out!*

"Today is a very special, extraordinary, surprising day." Juanita can't think of any more adjectives to say about today. She is only in third grade.

"Today . . . ," Miguel picks up, but he, too, draws a blank. Seven in the morning is not his best time of day to be creative either.

But it is Mami's. "Oh, that's right! Now I remember. Today is Bring a Special Person or Object to School Day. Um, right?" Mami looks over at Miguel and Juanita, who are trying desperately not to giggle.

"And Juanita and I picked you to be that special

object—I mean, person." Miguel grins. He hopes Tía Lola understands he was just joking.

But Tía Lola is not grinning back. Instead, she looks long and hard at Miguel, then at Juanita, finally at Mami. Is this a trick? her eyes are asking. Finally, she slips off her apron and smooths back her hair. *"Buenas razones cautivan los corazones."*

Juanita isn't sure what Tía Lola has just said. But if they start translating and explaining, Tía Lola will never be on time for the bus. "So are you going to come with us, Tía Lola?"

"¿Hoy sólo?" Miguel adds. Just for today?

"Solamente hoy," Tía Lola corrects him. "You can also say *hoy solamente.*"

She'll do fine teaching Spanish at Bridgeport, Miguel is thinking. All Tía Lola needs is some confidence.

"Hoy solamente, solamente hoy," Juanita practices, showing off her perfect pronunciation. Miguel groans. Here's one person who doesn't need more confidence.

"I'll be right down. Let me quickly get dressed and touch up my face." Tía Lola hurries upstairs.

Miguel knows what his aunt is about to do. Her beauty mark is about to migrate to a different part of her face. Her outfit will be just as colorful as before, but it will be a dress instead of a robe. Her favorite yellow scarf will be tied around her neck. Inside her flowered carpetbag purse, she'll be carrying a bottle of lucky water to sprinkle in the classroom. Just as long as she doesn't walk down the halls, burning candles and herbs to chase away bad spirits.

Miguel sighs. It is going to be a very long day at Bridgeport Elementary.

● ● ●

"Was it okay to lie to Tía Lola?" Juanita worries out loud. Mami has just called Mrs. Stevens to let her know that Tía Lola will be coming to school today.

Miguel groans. His little sister *would* have to spoil their triumph by wondering if it was okay.

But Mami waves Juanita's worries away. "It's a little white lie, that's all."

Mami has explained how sometimes you have to tell a harmless untruth to spare someone's feelings. How it's okay to say that Mami is not home even though she is upstairs finishing a report due tomorrow and is not to be disturbed. Also, if Papi asks Miguel how he is doing, it's okay to say "just fine" when really Miguel feels sad that after months of separation, his parents are now divorced. He was hoping that they would change their minds and get back together again.

"You see, we're actually helping Tía Lola. She really needs to get out of the house."

"Can't she get a job?" Miguel suggests. Isn't that what grown-ups are supposed to do?

"Tía Lola does have a job here, helping take care of

you," Mami reminds him. In Vermont, there aren't tons of after-school programs like back in the city, or relatives like their *abuelitos* in Brooklyn, ready to drop everything to come take care of their grandchildren.

"I think we did the right thing." Mami glances up at the kitchen clock. "You better hurry and call Tía Lola to come down. After all, you don't want to miss the bus on her first visit to Bridgeport."

As Juanita and Miguel are hurrying to gather their things together, Miguel remembers something he wanted to ask his mother. "Do you think Tía Lola knows we've told her a little white lie about it being a special day at Bridgeport?" After all, if they're going to have to pretend, they'd better know what they're in for.

Mami considers for a moment, drying her hands slowly and more thoroughly than usual. "Actually, Tía Lola said something that makes me suspect she knows we have something up our sleeves," Mami explains. "*Buenas razones cautivan los corazones.* Good intentions win hearts. She realizes we're all trying to make her feel less lonely, and that has won her over. Even though she's a little scared, she is willing to go with you to Bridgeport."

"But only for today, right?" Miguel asks. He doesn't mind giving in to his good intentions if it's just for this one time.

lesson two

En el país de los ciegos, el tuerto es rey
In the land of the blind, the one-eyed man is king

On her first day at school, Tía Lola is a huge hit.

Before the bus has pulled into the parking lot, Tía Lola has taught everyone to sing "*Pollito,* chicken; *gallina,* hen," a catchy rhyme that helps you learn words in English and Spanish. "*Lápiz,* pencil; *pluma,* pen."

When they arrive, Mrs. Stevens is at the door, shaking hands with each and every student.

Tía Lola has no way of knowing that Mrs. Stevens begins every day this way. She thinks that the principal is giving everyone a special welcome because today is Bring a Special Person or Object to School Day. Tía Lola

13

has yet to ask Miguel or Juanita why she seems to be the only visitor.

"I'm so glad you agreed to come." Mrs. Stevens shakes Tía Lola's hand vigorously. And Tía Lola doesn't just shake back. She throws her arms around the principal and gives her a great big hug. And Mrs. Stevens, who is very proper, laughs!

"That's a Spanish hug. *Un abrazo.*" Tía Lola tells Miguel to translate.

"Un abrazo," the principal practices. "How do you say 'Welcome to Bridgeport'?" Mrs. Stevens asks Miguel and Juanita.

"Bienvenida a Bridgeport," Tía Lola pipes right up. It's as if she can understand English once she has become friends.

Mrs. Stevens tries the phrase several times until Tía Lola cries out, *"¡Excelente!"* which sounds enough like "excellent" that Miguel and Juanita don't have to translate for the principal.

●●●

Mrs. Stevens suggests that Tía Lola start by visiting Juanita's class, and then Miguel's. That way, their aunt can get acquainted with the schedule and the layout of the school before she is on her own in the other classes.

"This is Tía Lola." Juanita introduces her aunt to her combined second-and-third-grade class and their teacher, Ms. Sweeney. " *'Tía'* means 'aunt' in Spanish."

From her seat in the circle of chairs, Ofie nods proudly, like she and Juanita invented Spanish all by themselves.

Milton raises his hand. He always has a question. If someone ran into the room and yelled, "Fire!" Milton would probably raise his hand and ask where the fire was and what could have caused it.

"Milton, do you have a question?" Ms. Sweeney asks nicely, as if there's ever a question that Milton has a question.

"What are we supposed to call her, since she's not our aunt?"

Ms. Sweeney turns to Juanita. "Can you ask your aunt what she'd like us to call her?"

Juanita thinks she already knows the answer, but she asks anyway. "My aunt says she wants to be Tía Lola to all my friends," Juanita translates when Tía Lola answers.

Milton raises his hand.

"Does anyone else have a question?" Ms. Sweeney looks around the room. No one does. She nods at Milton.

"What if we're not friends with Juanita . . . yet?" Milton asks.

For a moment, before Milton adds "yet," a worry line travels across Ms. Sweeney's forehead. This is only her first year teaching, and so she tries very hard to see that everything goes smoothly, which can make for a bumpy ride. "That's right, Milton," she says, relieved. "Everyone at Bridgeport is either a friend or a soon-to-be friend. Tía Lola it will be!" She smiles at Tía Lola, who plants a

15

big kiss on Ms. Sweeney's cheek, as if they have been friends forever.

●●●

Ms. Sweeney asks the class if they have any questions for Tía Lola. This time, not just Milton's hand shoots up.

"Where is the Dominican?" Chelsea wants to know.

"Anyone know, besides Juanita?" Ms. Sweeney asks. She is probably thinking Juanita has raised her hand because she knows the answer. But Juanita just wants to explain that the name of the country is the Dominican REPUBLIC, not the Dominican. After all, you wouldn't call the United States the United!

Ms. Sweeney calls on Ofie, who guesses that the Dominican Republic is near Mexico.

"Close enough," Ms. Sweeney says nicely, pulling down the rolled-up map above the blackboard.

Tía Lola's face lights up when she sees her little dot of a country, south of Florida, floating on the ocean. She touches the spot and calls out, *"¡Cierren los ojos y abran su imaginación!"*

"Shut your eyes and open your imagination!" Juanita translates.

Suddenly—or does Juanita imagine this?—the room fills with screeching parrots. Ocean waves crash against the blackboard, and jungle flowers press against the steamed-up windows. The sun is warm on her skin, and her feet sink into soft sand. All around, Juanita hears her classmates talking in Spanish. Oh my! Juanita knows her aunt is special, but this *is* extraordinary, and totally surprising.

"*¡Ya!*" Tía Lola claps her hands. Juanita pulls herself away from this tropical wonderland. Her classmates are also rubbing their eyes and shaking their heads. Everyone looks slightly tanned, and extremely impressed. Even Milton is silenced, though his mouth is wide open in wonder. Hannah, a quiet, usually shy girl, speaks for them all when she says, "That was . . . awesome!"

At the door, Miguel has arrived to escort Tía Lola to his classroom.

"*Adiós,* Tía Lola!" the children call out. "When are you coming back?" It's not every day they get to have such an amazing visitor.

"The next time you have a Special Visitor Day," Tía Lola says, and tells her niece to translate.

Juanita and Miguel exchange a look. Their little white lie is getting bigger and darker.

●●●

Tía Lola is thoughtful as she and her nephew walk down the hall. "Why didn't your sister translate what I just said?"

Is this the time to tell Tía Lola the truth? Miguel wonders. But if he tells her now, it might ruin her visit to his class. The end of the school day will be soon enough.

"I think maybe Juanita was having such a great time, she forgot to translate," Miguel says, which is sort of true. In fact, when Miguel had opened the door, the whole class seemed to be in a trance. He himself had felt a blast of warm, sunny air on his face. Not only that, he thought he'd heard parrots! Parrots in Vermont, in the middle of winter?! It was like that classroom was under a spell. "You didn't work some magic in there, did you?" Miguel asks his aunt bluntly.

Tía Lola laughs and shakes her head. *"No hice nada."* She didn't do a thing. The children just used their imaginations.

"Fifth graders have really great imaginations," Miguel brags. He wants to be sure Tía Lola understands that she is moving up in the world. From third to fifth grade is an enormous leap. It's like going from being an ape to being a human being. In his imagination, Miguel sees Juanita suddenly turning hairy, with a long tail coming out of her dress. He can't help but laugh.

Tía Lola looks over at him as if she knows exactly what he is thinking.

Suddenly, Miguel can see *himself* transformed into a big, dumb orangutan. Quickly, he turns his sister back to her normal self in his imagination. Lo and behold, he can see himself turning back into a boy. He slows his steps. He wants to be sure that the change is complete before he faces a room full of his classmates.

●●●

Mrs. Prouty, the teacher for the combined fourth and fifth grades, has already met Tía Lola a number of times in town. They kiss like old friends. Tía Lola asks after Mrs. Prouty's *gorditas,* which Miguel can't really translate, as it's not really polite to call his teacher's twin daughters fatties. His mother has explained that Tía Lola actually means the word as a compliment. Back on the island, where a lot of people are so poor, being chubby means your family is well-off. But here in the United States, it would be a mean thing to say.

"Tía Lola wants to know how your daughters are," Miguel translates.

Mrs. Prouty's face turns pink with pleasure. They are very well, thank you, taking skating lessons, eager to start middle school in September. Throughout this exchange, Miguel is busy with the back-and-forth translation. He hopes Tía Lola soon picks up English and his teachers and classmates learn Spanish, or he will be working extra hard from now on. Hey, maybe he can get paid for his services? Now, that would be awesome: earning money like an adult while going to school like a kid.

"Miguel?" Mrs. Prouty is asking. "What would your *tía* Lola like to do for her first day as our Spanish teacher?"

Oh no! Miguel can't really translate what his teacher has asked or Tía Lola will realize she has been tricked. One good thing about being the only one in his class who knows Spanish is that he doesn't have to translate exactly what Mrs. Prouty says and get into trouble.

"What do you want to do today, *solamente hoy*?" Miguel asks his aunt in Spanish.

"I am your special *object*!" She winks at Miguel, which is embarrassing in front of all his classmates. "And so whatever you want me to do on this Bring a Special Person or Object to School Day, *estoy a tus órdenes.*" I am at your service.

"Whatever you want her to do," Miguel pretends to translate.

"My oh my!" Mrs. Prouty scratches her head. "It sure takes a lot more words to say something in Spanish than in English. Tell your aunt that we would love for her to tell us a little bit about what lies ahead for us in Spanish class. Will we need any special materials, say?"

Miguel is sweating bullets! How to translate and still not let Tía Lola know she is now their Spanish teacher? Miguel might not look like a dumb orangutan, but he sure feels like one right this moment.

"What did your teacher say?" Tía Lola prompts him.

Miguel looks up at his aunt. Her eyes are full of love and forgiveness. Good intentions win hearts, he reminds himself. He hopes Tía Lola will forgive him when he finally tells her the truth. "My teacher wants to know how our class can learn some Spanish."

"How?" Tía Lola looks surprised by the question. "Why, I can teach them! It is so much easier than English."

"Tía Lola says you don't need any special materials because Spanish is so much easier than English." Miguel wipes the sweat from his forehead.

20

"Oh, I don't know about that," Mrs. Prouty says. "Anyhow, if you would tell your aunt . . ."

Miguel glances up at the clock. Fifteen minutes down and fifteen more to go before he can translate the one word that will free him from this big, dark, messy lie: *¡Adiós!* Tía Lola says goodbye!

●●●

"How was school today?" Mami asks before even taking her coat off. They are the first words out of her mouth when she gets home from work.

"Muy, muy bien," Tía Lola says, smiling broadly. "But the most curious thing: I was the only guest in the whole school."

Miguel has been waiting for this moment all day. It's time to tell Tía Lola the truth. "We didn't mean to lie to you," he begins.

"We had good intentions," Juanita adds. "And everybody in my class just loved your visit! They want you to come back."

"Let me, children," Mami intervenes. "It's really my fault, Tía Lola. I was the one who encouraged them. I knew you'd be great. You just needed to get over worrying about not knowing enough to teach the children. Didn't I tell you that they'd love you?"

Tía Lola looks around at all of them, a loving, forgiving smile on her face. "I didn't tell you the whole truth either," she admits to Miguel and Juanita. "Your

21

mami knows how very poor our family was. We lived way out in the *campo,* in the middle of nowhere. So I didn't get much schooling. I didn't even advance to your grade, Miguel. I meant to go back. In fact, when my older sister died . . ." Miguel and Juanita know that part of the story. Mami's parents died when Mami was a little girl, and her aunt Lola moved to the capital to take care of her. "In the city, I started night school. But I couldn't keep attending."

Mami reaches for Tía Lola's hand and squeezes it gratefully. Tía Lola is not saying so, but she was working long hours as a seamstress and also taking care of her little niece. She had no extra time to be a student.

"I have had a beautiful life." Tía Lola wants to be sure Mami and her little niece and nephew know she is not complaining. "But I haven't had much schooling. So you see, I didn't want to embarrass you by being dumb in front of your friends."

"But you know so much more Spanish than any of us, Tía Lola," Juanita reminds her aunt.

"That's the lesson *I* learned today!" Tía Lola laughs. *"En el país de los ciegos, el tuerto es rey."*

"In the land of the blind, the one-eyed man is king," Mami translates. Miguel and Juanita still don't get it, so Mami explains. "A one-eyed man doesn't have perfect vision, but he sees a lot more than a blind man. Sometimes, if you know just a little bit about something that no one around you knows anything about, you get to be the leader. And Tía Lola actually knows a lot of Spanish in a place where hardly anyone knows a word of it."

"I get it," Juanita says in her know-it-all voice. "So Tía Lola is like the king."

"You mean she is like the queen, *la reina*." Miguel smirks back at his little sister.

"Reina Lola!" Queen Lola claps her hands, delighted.

For a brief moment, Miguel sees a gold crown sitting on Tía Lola's head. He rubs his eyes. Fifth graders sure have an overactive imagination—from ape boys to queen aunts. . . .

lesson three

Camarón que se duerme se lo lleva la corriente
The sleeping shrimp is carried away by the current

Juanita's head is in the clouds. She sits in her third-grade classroom, riding a unicorn from medieval times. She tries to add all the numbers on the board and ends up going down a sixty-foot rabbit hole. She gets up to answer a question and is suddenly airborne on a magic carpet, headed for the sultan's court. But wait . . . someone is calling her name.

"Juanita! Earth to Juanita!" Ms. Sweeney is saying. The class laughs. Juanita's face burns. She knows her very nice teacher would never purposely embarrass her. Neither does she, Juanita, mean to be rude in any way.

24

A little later, Ms. Sweeney goes from desk to desk, checking on each student's penmanship exercise. But Juanita has not finished even the first line. She was just now trying to escape from forty thieves and having a very hard time riding on a camel.

At afternoon recess, Ms. Sweeney asks Juanita to stay behind for a few minutes after everyone has gone out. "Is something wrong, Juanita? Everything okay at home?"

Juanita shakes her head that nothing is wrong, then nods that everything is okay at home.

"I thought your aunt was going to start teaching us Spanish." It has been a week since Tía Lola's visit.

"She's practicing," Juanita explains. "She says she has to learn a lot more if she expects to be a one-eyed queen in the land of the blind."

Ms. Sweeney smiles uncertainly. "I see," she says at last. But even if Juanita had only one eye, she'd see that Ms. Sweeney doesn't understand what Juanita means at all.

●●●

How does Juanita convince her teacher that she is not having a problem?

In fact, a super, fantastic, extraordinarily wonderful thing has happened: Juanita has fallen in love with reading! Of course, she has been reading for ages, like since kindergarten, but it was always hard work, sounding out words and stuff. But now reading is her favorite thing in the world! She looks at a page and the words all link

25

together, and it's like a string of Christmas lights that come on when you replace the one little bulb that wasn't working.

The words make up sentences, and the sentences take her deeper and deeper inside a story. Once she gets started, Juanita can't stop. The story keeps going and pulling her along even after she has closed the book. She sits in the classroom, daydreaming.

"Juanita!" Ms. Sweeney is calling her again.

Slowly, Juanita descends on her hot-air balloon. She has been around the world in eighty days and has so much to tell, but all Ms. Sweeney wants to know are the names of the states bordering Idaho.

❋❋❋

Ms. Sweeney sends a note home with Juanita. Mami tears open the envelope and reads, the little line between her eyebrows deepening.

"Am I in trouble?" Juanita wants to know. But her *mami* just looks at her daughter closely before shaking her head slowly.

"Is Ms. Sweeney upset that I forgot to finish my homework?" This has been happening a lot, but Mami doesn't need to know the exact number of times.

"It's nothing." Mami folds the letter and puts it back in the envelope, then gives Juanita a brave smile.

"Is it about not sharing my animals?" Juanita tries again. One day last week, Juanita took her two stuffed

26

dinosaurs to school, but she wouldn't let anyone play with them because they were actually keeping her company as she flew in a magic tree house back to prehistoric times.

"No, *amorcito*, love. I told you, it's nothing."

"But it's got to be about something, Mami," Juanita protests.

Mami hesitates. Then, out of the blue, she asks Juanita, "You're not worried about . . . the divorce or anything?"

Juanita shakes her head. Of course, she wishes her parents hadn't divorced. But Juanita hasn't been worried about it or anything else until right now, when her *mami* won't tell her what's in her teacher's letter.

"Well, then, let's not start worrying about a silly note." Mami laughs a phony laugh that doesn't convince Juanita at all.

"So is it about arguing with Ofie?" Juanita persists. After Tía Lola's visit, Juanita and Ofie had a disagreement about who spoke the best Spanish, Mexicans or Dominicans.

Mami shakes her head again. At this rate, Mami is going to find out all of Juanita's secrets before Juanita ever learns what is in Ms. Sweeney's letter.

● ● ●

Juanita finds Tía Lola in her attic room, hunched over her Spanish books. Every night after supper, Tía Lola has been excusing herself and going upstairs to study. She

27

has to learn lots more before she can begin teaching. It used to be that Tía Lola would think up such fun things to do, like putting on Dominican music and teaching Juanita and her *mami* some hip-swirling dance steps. Or she'd tell one of her wonderful stories that were as good as opening up a favorite chapter book and reading about some adventure. Or, if Rudy came over, they'd make piñatas to hang in his restaurant in the shape of every animal imaginable.

Now all Tía Lola wants to do is cram her head full of information so she'll be smart enough to teach in school.

But the minute Tía Lola spots her niece at the door, she closes her books. *"¿Qué hay, Juanita?"* she asks. No matter how busy she is, Tía Lola always has time to ask how her little niece is doing.

Juanita explains that her teacher sent a letter home. "I think Ms. Sweeney is upset with me. But Mami won't tell me exactly why. Maybe Mami'll tell you?" Juanita looks up hopefully.

"She might. But then she might not. Or she might tell me but then make me promise not to tell." Tía Lola is half talking to Juanita and half talking to herself. She narrows her eyes as if the answer to this problem is so far away, she has to look hard to spot it. Finally, she does. "I think the only solution is for me to start my Spanish classes. That way, if there is a *problema* in your class, I will help *la señorita* Sweeney solve it."

With her aunt there, Juanita will surely climb back

28

into Ms. Sweeney's good graces. Besides, Juanita is going to make an extra-special effort not to be distracted by the stories in her head. It's the least she can do to show Tía Lola how grateful she is for coming to her aid like a medieval knight in one of Juanita's favorite books.

●●●

Tía Lola is welcomed back with clapping and cheers. Her colorful clothes brighten up the gray winter day. Her smile is contagious. And she has come up with the best lesson plan ever: a Spanish treasure hunt!

First, they'll spend several weeks learning all the words and phrases that will appear as clues. Then, on the day of the hunt, during their morning recess, Tía Lola and Ms. Sweeney will hide clues all over the room. Whichever team finds the card that says *"tesoro"* will be the winner of a special surprise Tía Lola will bring to class.

Milton's hand goes up, but Tía Lola has a way of figuring out his questions before he even asks them. *"Tesoro,"* she says, writing the word on the board.

Ofie calls out, "It means 'treasure.' "

"But what is the treasure going to be?" Milton wants to know.

"¡Una sorpresa!" Tía Lola answers.

"It's going to be a surprise," Ofie translates.

A surprise treasure for the winning team. Wow! The whole class breaks out again in spontaneous clapping.

"Why can't school always be this fun?" Milton asks. He has not raised his hand, but then, this is not really a question.

Ms. Sweeney's forehead does not wrinkle up at this complaint. She has been so relaxed since Tía Lola started coming to her class. In fact, the two teachers huddle together in the front of the room, planning and plotting. Amazingly, each one seems to understand what the other is saying without a whole lot of translating.

●●●

For weeks on end, Tía Lola goes over Spanish vocabulary and sayings, mostly without Juanita's help. Oh, sometimes Juanita will pitch in when she's not too busy daydreaming.

Every night after supper, Tía Lola locks herself in her bedroom in order to work on the surprise treasure. It's okay, because Juanita has a lot of reading to do before Mami makes her turn off the lights.

Finally, the day of the hunt arrives.

"So remember," Ms. Sweeney reminds the class. "You'll be divided into two teams. The second-grade team will be led by Ofie, the third-grade team by Juanita." Much cheering and clapping.

Juanita is pulled back to the classroom. What just happened? She'd better not ask or Ms. Sweeney will know that Juanita has not been paying attention. How could she, when she has been standing in a huge crowd,

30

watching the emperor parade by without any clothes and wondering if she should speak out?

"Since they both know Spanish, they can help their teams with the clues and rules," Ms. Sweeney concludes.

Juanita is supposed to be the leader of her team and she isn't even sure how the game works! She'll be a blind queen in the land of the one-eyed! When Milton's hand goes up, Juanita secretly hopes that her classmate has a question about the rules so that Ms. Sweeney will have to go over them one more time.

But Milton has been listening carefully for weeks. In fact, every day he greets Juanita with *"Hola, Juanita. ¿Cómo estás?"* instead of "Hello! How are you?" Yesterday, he actually hollered, *"¡Hola, camarón!"* Juanita didn't have a clue what a *camarón* was. She had meant to ask Tía Lola when they got home, but she forgot.

"What is it, Milton?" Ms. Sweeney asks.

"When can we *empezar*?" Milton grins.

Ms. Sweeney grins back. "We can start right after recess!"

●●●

After recess, the treasure hunt starts. Ofie and her team of second graders zip around the room, unearthing one clue after another.

Juanita's team lags behind. When they stumble over words, their leader, Juanita, can't help them out. Tía Lola has been reviewing words and sayings for weeks with her class, but Juanita hasn't been paying attention. She thought she didn't have to because she already knew tons of Spanish. Instead, she has been living in a boxcar and wondering what on earth she and her sister and brothers will have for dinner.

And so it is no surprise that Ofie's team is the first to reach the last clue: *Camarón que se duerme se lo lleva la corriente.* "The shrimp who falls asleep is carried away by the current," Ofie translates. People who don't pay attention lose out on real-life adventures.

Right off, Ofie's team figures out where the treasure card is hidden: in Juanita's desk! It seems everyone knows Juanita has not been paying attention in class.

No wonder Milton has been calling her *camarón*. Juanita has been carried away by the current of her daydreaming.

But now she is wide awake, listening to the other team's triumphant shouts. Juanita wishes a strong current would carry her away so she doesn't have to face the disappointment of her teammates. Especially when Tía Lola unveils the winners' prize: a big donkey piñata filled with candies and stickers and dollar-store trinkets, which Ofie's team will break open in the art room after lunch.

❋❋❋

For the rest of the school day, Juanita feels miserable. There is no thought of princesses or emperors or dragons. No magic tree houses, boxcars, dinosaur rides, swans laying golden eggs, princesses in towers. The only scene playing over and over in her head is that moment of losing the treasure hunt.

Juanita can't wait to get home so she can have a good cry with all her dolls and stuffed animals and books to comfort her. Except she knows that nothing can take away her bitter disappointment with herself. She has let down her teammates, Ms. Sweeney, and most of all, Tía Lola, who actually put aside her fear of teaching to come help Juanita get back into her teacher's good graces.

"I'm sorry, Tía Lola," Juanita apologizes to her aunt as they walk down the driveway once the bus has dropped them off. "I didn't mean to ignore everyone. It's just that I love reading. And I keep thinking about the stories once I put the books away."

Even though Tía Lola didn't get much schooling, she loves stories, so she understands. "If you keep loving books and stories so much, Juanita, maybe one day you can write your own stories."

Thinking about such a possibility takes away a tiny bit of Juanita's disappointment. Someday, if she writes wonderful books, maybe her teammates will forgive her.

"But remember, you have to have adventures in order to have stories to tell," Tía Lola says wisely. "So you have to pay attention to all the wonderful things happening in your own life."

This is just the boost Juanita needs. Tomorrow, she will apologize to her whole class and tell them she is ready for some real-life adventures with them as her companions and Ms. Sweeney and Tía Lola as their guides.

"I just wish I could make it up to my team," Juanita confesses to Tía Lola, who comes up with a wonderful idea. Why not make a losers' piñata? Juanita can pick whatever animal she wants it to be.

All weekend long, Tía Lola and Juanita work on the losers' piñata. On Monday, Mami drives them both to school, as Tía Lola wants to be there for the surprise. From the trunk, Juanita pulls out the fat pink shrimp piñata for her losing team.

"Hola . . . ," Milton calls across the parking lot to Juanita. But before he can say *"camarón"* his mouth drops open. "What in the world is that?"

"It's a *camarón,"* Juanita says, already feeling a lot better. "It was carried away by the current, but we caught it and are bringing it back."

lesson four

Con paciencia y con calma,
se subió un burro en una palma
With patience and calm,
even a donkey can climb a palm

Miguel is in a big hurry.

He wants to race through fifth and sixth grade and be in middle school, away from his annoying little sister at Bridgeport Elementary.

He wants to be in the major leagues, old enough so he doesn't have to ask his parents' permission to sign on with the Yankees.

He is impatient with how short he is. Okay, so he's not the shortest boy in his class (which includes fourth

35

graders, after all). But of all the fifth graders, only Oliver and Lily are shorter, and there are three fourth graders who are actually taller than Miguel—and one of them, Anna, is even a girl. Miguel's mother keeps telling him that one day he will probably be as tall as his *papi,* but Miguel doesn't want to have to get there in inches. That could take years!

When they first moved to Vermont, Miguel wanted to have instant friends, instant good feelings about the place. He was impatient for everything to be great right away! But instead, for months on end, he was horribly homesick. He missed the city. He missed the Yankees. He missed his best friend, José, and his old school. But most of all, he missed Papi.

Now, a year later, Miguel has made new friends. His classmates have stopped teasing him about his name, Guzmán ("Gooseman"), and asking silly questions about being Hispanic. Besides, they can now ask Tía Lola. Everybody loves Spanish class and looks forward to the two days a week, Tuesday and Thursday—that is, *martes y jueves*—when Tía Lola officially comes to school. But many other days, by popular demand, Tía Lola drops in to help with other projects. Miguel has to admit that his aunt is fun to have around.

But one thing that has never, ever gotten easier is the separation from his *papi.* While he's in New York, Miguel is impatient to get back to Vermont. He misses his new friends, his big rented house in the country, and especially his *mami.* But every time Miguel comes back from a visit with his father, he is impatient for the next time.

More immediately, Miguel is impatient with his reading problem. Wouldn't you know it—just as his little sister is becoming what she calls a voracious reader, Miguel is lagging behind in English class. It's so hard to get through a sentence with so many little stumbling blocks: words he doesn't know (like "voracious"), meanings he doesn't get ("In the land of the blind, the one-eyed man is king"). Miguel wishes he could be really good in English class right away.

"Maybe having two languages has confused him?" Mrs. Prouty suggests to Mami during parent-teacher conferences.

"Nonsense!" Mami says later, on the ride home. "Juanita has two languages, most of Europe speaks two or three languages. . . ."

Great. Now Miguel is not just dumber than his little sister, but dumber than a whole continent!

While Tía Lola and Mami and Juanita chatter away, Miguel looks out his window. Snowy fields spread out on either side of the road. There's nothing to take his mind off his remedial status at school. He feels impatient to get home, but once there, what next? Homework, and nagging from his mother, and pestering from his little sister . . .

It's going to be a long night. Miguel sighs impatiently.

***

Later that night, as Miguel sits down to do his homework, the phone rings. It's Papi. He has something he wants to discuss with Miguel and his little sister, but he wants to do it in person.

Oh no. Miguel's heart fills with dread. The last few times Miguel and Juanita have visited Papi, Carmen, Papi's girlfriend, has always hung out with them. Not that there's anything wrong with Carmen, who is perfectly nice and friendly and sort of pretty. It's just that Miguel doesn't want anybody to be married to his *papi* except his *mami*.

"Car and I, we're thinking of heading up this next weekend to see you. It's too long to wait till you come down for winter recess in February," Papi is explaining. Miguel loves hearing that Papi wants to visit. But why does he have to spoil it by saying "we"? Lots of times, after he finishes talking to Miguel, Papi says, "Car wants to say hi," and Miguel is stuck answering a bunch of stupid questions about how school is going and when practice is starting up for his Little League team. But today, instead of putting Car on, his *papi* says, "Let me talk to your mother, *mi'jo.*" When Papi calls Miguel *mi'jo,* meaning "my son," it's usually because he's got something serious and parental on his mind.

After a few cool hellos and how-are-yous, Mami's face gets an alert, private look. "Hold on," she says, and with her hand over the speaker, she asks Miguel if he wouldn't mind giving her some space. The last words Miguel can make out as the kitchen door is closing are

38

"Yes, I can talk now." And then something-something-something, which just by Mami's tone Miguel can tell is not the good kind of something he should be looking forward to.

Miguel heads upstairs to alert his little sister about the upcoming visit. She's not in her room, but he finds her up in the attic, in Tía Lola's bedroom. They are designing a piñata as a gift for Rudy's birthday. Oh no! The surprise party is this Saturday! Miguel considers racing downstairs to remind Mami. But then Papi will have to reschedule his visit, and Miguel will have to wait a whole other week or two, or maybe even till winter recess, to find out the something-something-something that his *papi* has to tell him in person. If it's bad news, Miguel is impatient to get his heartache over and done with.

● ● ●

The very next day, at dinner, Tía Lola mentions Rudy's birthday party on Saturday.

"*Ay*, no!" Mami wails. "I'd completely forgotten!" She hurries to the phone even though they're in the middle of eating. "I better call your father and tell him not to come."

Nobody answers at the apartment. Mami leaves a message, but she is almost one hundred percent sure Papi has already set out. "He talked about taking off for a long weekend." She looks over at Miguel and Juanita, as if they are on a sinking ship and she is trying to figure out how to save them. "I guess it won't be the end of the world," she says glumly.

I hope not, Miguel feels like saying. But then, his mother knows a lot more than he does about why his father is coming this weekend. What could be so bad that his mother should even think of comparing it to the end of the world?

"I know!" Juanita's face lights up. "Papi can come to Rudy's party!"

"I'm sure Rudy wouldn't mind if we invited Daniel," Tía Lola agrees.

"That would be so great!" Juanita is pumping her body up and down in her seat like a piston in a car engine. "He'll get to see my piñata, Tía Lola!"

Miguel is almost sure that his little sister hasn't a clue what Papi might be planning. But even if she does, Juanita has never questioned Carmen's presence in Papi's life. As far as Juanita is concerned, she's got her New York City best friend, Ming, just as Miguel has José, and so why shouldn't Papi have Carmen? That way, they can each have somebody special to hold hands with when they go to the zoo or to a ball game or to Brooklyn, to their *abuelitos'* apartment.

"Daniel's not coming alone," Mami says in a tight voice, looking over at Tía Lola. Miguel watches his aunt's face. It's like a sunrise, the slow dawning of a new day—or in this case, of the realization that Papi's new life is about to land on their doorstep.

Rudy's surprise party at his own restaurant is, of course, Tía Lola's idea. This will be his sixtieth birthday, but he refuses to take the day off. "Why should I?" Rudy protests. "This is the funnest place to be on my birthday!"

"So we'll just have his party at the *restaurante*," Tía Lola decides. The only problem is trying to keep it a secret from Rudy.

All week long, anyone who has called for a reservation on Saturday has been invited to a party instead. Since it's usually Shauna or Dawn answering calls, Rudy has no idea that this Saturday there's going to be a big surprise fiesta at his restaurant. Juanita is making a donkey piñata with Tía Lola's help. That is the best animal for a piñata, Juanita informs Miguel in her know-it-all voice.

"Donkey piñatas are totally boring," Miguel informs her back in his know-it-all voice.

"No, they're not! My piñata is real special."

"Actually, you're right," Miguel says, pretending to change his mind. "I don't think I've ever seen a donkey piñata that looks so much like a chicken. Now, that *is* special."

"It does *not* look like a chicken!" Juanita protests. Then she appeals to their aunt: "Does my piñata look like a chicken, Tía Lola?"

"It looks like a beautiful yellow donkey with a pointy nose," Tía Lola assures her. Somehow that makes both children happy.

Tonight they are working in the kitchen so that Tía Lola can help with the piñatas while also minding the baking she's doing for the party. She has already finished several batches of *suspiros,* cookies whose name means "sighs" because they are light and airy but (sigh!) gone before you know it. Also a tin full of *caballitos,* "little horses," cookies with a kick of ginger. The kitchen smells delicious. Meanwhile, on the table, there are piles of bright tissue paper and a jar of paste and a pail of paint-brushes as well as chicken wire to make the frames on which to drape the strips of paper into a credible animal.

"So what are you going to make?" Juanita challenges her brother, who has been doodling another page of ze-roes in his notebook.

Miguel shrugs like he doesn't care. But in fact, he can't seem to come up with any ideas at all for a cool piñata. He is starting to feel like a total loser, and not just in English class. When his little sister heads upstairs with Mami for her bedtime, Tía Lola sits down across the table from Miguel.

"*¿Qué hay, Miguel?*" she asks. How is her nephew doing?

Miguel sighs and closes his notebook. "I feel like I'm not good at anything." He is ready to admit it—out of earshot of his sister.

"Of course you are. You're a good baseball player," Tía Lola reminds him kindly. "You have a great imagi-nation. You're good with your hands. You have green fin-gers, like the Americans say."

"It's thumbs, Tía Lola, green thumbs," Miguel corrects her. All last summer, Miguel did help Tía Lola with her vegetable garden, which she insisted on planting in the shape of the Dominican Republic. Actually, all he did was follow her directions. "And I'm not exactly good at any of those things, Tía Lola, just average. And lately, below average."

"Con paciencia y con calma, se subió un burro en una palma," Tía Lola counsels. It's a little rhyme that makes Miguel smile in spite of his impatience: "With patience and calm, even a donkey can climb a palm." In his imagination, Miguel sees a donkey struggling to get up a palm tree.

"The best ideas come when you relax and let your mind play," Tía Lola is saying. "So take a deep breath and count to ten."

Miguel does just that. When he is done counting, Tía Lola tells him to begin again! "This time, I want you to count to ten in Spanish. *Uno, dos* . . ." She talks Miguel through the exercise, reminding him to breathe between each number.

Just as they are getting to *diez,* ten, a flashbulb goes off in Miguel's brain. He has a great idea for a piñata: a palm tree to go along with his sister's donkey!

"What are you laughing at?" Mami has joined them in the kitchen after tucking in Juanita.

"Myself, I guess," Miguel says, and that's not a white lie either. Tía Lola has always said that a sense of humor is a sense of perspective. Now Miguel sort of knows what she means. Everything that seems worrisome and huge can suddenly look manageable and small if you take the time to be patient and see the humor in things. Like imagining that poor donkey struggling to climb up a palm tree.

●●●

By Friday, however, Miguel is feeling impatient again. He sits in school all day, wondering if Papi has already arrived in Vermont. He counts to ten and *diez* so many times, any donkey would have climbed up to the clouds by now.

In math, the long-division problems seem to go on forever. Afterward, it's science and how gravity works. Talk about *borrrring*! In social studies, the class is putting together a poster, titled IF YOU WERE THERE IN 1492: EVERYDAY LIFE IN THE TIME OF COLUMBUS. Who cares? Miguel thinks.

Then, after lunch, spelling, penmanship, and the dreaded reading period. By the time the final bell rings, Miguel is ready to bolt. But he still has to wait until his row is called. "One, *uno,* two, *dos* . . ." He practices being patient.

Finally, Miguel is saying goodbye to Mrs. Stevens at the front entrance. *"Feliz fin de semana, Miguel,"* she says, showing off her Spanish.

"Happy weekend, Mrs. Stevens," Miguel replies.

Out in the parking lot, Miguel scans the cars for out-of-state license plates. None in sight. But here's his little sister racing to join him, full of happy chatter about the weekend. Miguel will have to wait some more to reach the top of his palm tree: seeing Papi.

At long last, the bus drops them off at their mailbox. And there it is—a car with New York plates sitting in their driveway. But instead of racing ahead to be the first to hug his father, Miguel slows his steps. That sense of dread is descending again, like a great big collapsed palm tree on his head.

"Hey, Papi's here!" Juanita has just now noticed the car. But before she can run off, Miguel stops her.

"Nita, I need to tell you something," he begins patiently, wanting to prepare his little sister. "It's about . . . well . . ." But Miguel can't think of a way to say it more gently, and he ends up blurting it out: "I'm almost sure Papi's going to marry Carmen."

But his sister shrugs as if she still doesn't seem to understand that Papi's remarriage means they will be getting a stepmother. Now, Miguel's not a big reader like Juanita. But anyone who has read even a handful of fairy tales knows stepmothers can be pretty evil.

"Carmen'll be our stepmother," he reminds her.

"Is that bad?" Juanita asks. The look on her face, as well as her question, sends a pang through Miguel's heart. He's been in such a hurry to grow up, but now he wishes he were still as sweet and innocent as his little sister. "I like Carmen, don't you?" she adds.

Miguel hates to admit it, but his annoying, not-as-creative-as-a-fifth-grader baby sister has just made him stop in his tracks. Slowed down, with patience and calm, Miguel realizes that he doesn't dislike Carmen. What's more, his father is a lot happier now than when he was all by himself. But it's Mami that Miguel worries about. Even though she has never said so, Miguel senses that his liking Carmen would upset his mother. After all, unlike Papi, Mami hasn't found someone new to love.

"Carmen's okay," Miguel admits to his little sister. "I just want to wait awhile before we get new families."

"Miguel Ángel Guzmán!" His little sister cocks her head, hands on her hips, just like Mami when she is confronting him. "I thought you were the one always in a big huge hurry." Word for word what Mami says!

"I am!" Miguel hollers, and starts racing down the driveway, his little sister at his heels. Whether or not he's ready for a stepmother, Miguel is impatient about one thing: seeing his father.

lesson five

Los tropezones hacen levantar los pies
Stumbling makes you pick up your feet

It's Saturday evening, almost time for Rudy's surprise birthday party. While they wait for Papi and Carmen to arrive from the bed-and-breakfast down the road so they can all drive over to the restaurant, Juanita and Miguel go up to Tía Lola's attic bedroom to visit with her. Miguel has a pressing question he can't ask Mami.

"Papi said he wanted to come up because he had something to tell us, but he hasn't told us anything," Miguel begins. On the bed beside him is Tía Lola's piñata, a flamingo with long, skinny legs and a droopy neck that makes it look like an ostrich wanting to hide its head in the sand. But there is no mistaking its pink flamingo color.

"Knowing your *papi,* he's probably waiting for the right moment," Tía Lola suggests. "And today's been so busy. First, going to your ballet class, Juanita, and then over to the slopes to watch you snowboard, Miguel. It has been a wonderful day, don't you think?" But Tía Lola doesn't wait for their answer. "Carmen is just so nice," she adds—unnecessarily, in Miguel's opinion. It has been great to have Papi around, period. But even he has to admit that he did appreciate Carmen's exclaiming that Miguel Ángel is such a wonderful athlete, and ohmygoodness! so brave to come down a steep mountain on a small board.

"She said my pliés were like a real ballerina's." Juanita stands up and executes a couple of graceful bends, holding on to the bedpost.

"Carmen was right!" Tía Lola claps approvingly. "The truth is, Carmen is a good visitor. Did you see how she gobbled up my *pastelitos* at lunch? She said they were the best she'd had in months."

"I love how she calls us by our whole names: Miguel Ángel and Juana Inés," Juanita says, pointing to her brother and to herself. "She says they're the best names on account of yours was the greatest painter and mine the greatest poet."

Something is beginning to bug Miguel like a pebble in his shoe: Carmen seems to be spreading her compliments around a little too generously. Does she really mean what she says, or is she just trying to be nice to everyone?

"You know what they say," Tía Lola says. She always seems to be able to read Miguel's thoughts. *"Más moscas se cogen con una gota de miel que con un cuarto de vinagre."* You catch more flies with a drop of honey than you do with a quart of vinegar.

Instead of Tía Lola's helping to shake the annoying pebble from Miguel's shoe, her saying adds another pebble. Who wants to think of himself as a duped fly?

Juanita has stopped her plié-ing to look squarely at her aunt. "Tía Lola, do you have a saying for everything?"

"Just about," Tía Lola says, laughing. "Now, let's get downstairs. You know what they say—"

"I know, I know," Juanita pipes up. " 'The shrimp who falls asleep is carried away by the current.' And that goes for flamingos, too," she adds, picking up Tía Lola's piñata by the loop in its center. The flamingo dangles from her hand, its neck and legs boinging up and down. It looks like it is trying to dance the merengue, which is hard to do with a tennis ball knotted at each knee and two others holding down its feet.

"On the other hand," Miguel offers, " 'waking up early doesn't make the sun rise any faster.' "

"Right!" Juanita gives her brother a high five. "So we might as well 'dress slowly if we're in a hurry' "—another saying of Tía Lola's.

Their aunt stands before them in her bright floral dress, shaking her head at her niece and nephew. "You

49

two don't need to go to a party. You're having such a good time already!"

"That's because we love you, Tía Lola," Juanita says, just to make sure her aunt doesn't take offense at their teasing. "Don't we, Mr. Flamingo?" The pink bird bobs, agreeing with everything. Kind of like Carmen, Miguel can't help thinking.

❋❋❋

As they drive over to the party, a soft, celebratory snow begins to fall. Already the parking lot is full of cars—the whole town must be here. The invitation that Mami and Tía Lola sent out instructed everyone to congregate in the library parking lot at five-thirty. A few folks are selected to go across the street into the restaurant ahead of the others, like regular clients, just so Rudy doesn't get suspicious. Then, as planned, Dawn calls Rudy into the kitchen to help with some "emergency." Shauna blinks the lights, and that's the signal! Everyone hurries over—potluck platters and baskets stuffed with homemade goodies and other gifts in hand. When Rudy comes out of the kitchen, scratching his head, the dining room is packed with well-wishers yelling "SURPRISE!"

Except for Tía Lola, who is yelling *"¡SORPRESA!"*

Meanwhile, at the back door of the restaurant, a van has pulled up. Woody, Rudy's son, unloads several flats of sodas and pizzas and ice cream he couldn't deliver beforehand since his dad might catch on. In the front

50

dining room, the party is in full swing. From the ceiling hang three outstanding piñatas: a flourishing palm tree— nice to spot one in Vermont in winter; a jittery flamingo; and a donkey that looks a little henpecked. Trays of finger foods make the rounds. Tía Lola's *pastelitos* are gone so quickly that Carmen doesn't even get the chance to have one. "Oh well," she says graciously. "I already pigged out at lunch."

There are speeches and toasts. Everyone wants to know if Rudy didn't suspect that something was going on.

"I guess I'm getting old or something," Rudy says, laughing. "I didn't have the slightest. I did think supplies looked kind of low for a Saturday night. And when this one," he adds, pointing to his grinning son, "when he didn't show up on time, I was ready to fire him."

"Fire me?!" Woody says, pretending to be indignant. In the summer, he has a business putting up tents for outdoor weddings and receptions. In the winter, he's a ski bum, waitering some for his dad. It was his idea to order out most of the food—so that Rudy and all his staff could take the night off and enjoy themselves. But as the guest list grew, Mami and Tía Lola worriedly added "potluck" to the party invitation. Now there will be enough leftovers to feed the whole town for the rest of the week.

The cake comes out—a replica of Rudy's restaurant, with a white picket fence around the border formed by his sixty candles.

Everyone sings "Happy Birthday." Except for Tía Lola,

who sings *"Feliz Cumpleaños,"* which is the same song, only in Spanish. Then, after a bunch of people remind Rudy to make a wish and another bunch remind him not to tell anyone his wish or it won't come true, everyone insists that he give a speech.

"I'm not much on public speaking," Rudy begs off, but his guests are insistent.

Finally, he gives in. "Okay, okay! Where to start? Let's see. As some of you know, it's now almost six years since Rita died. . . ."

Rudy's voice has gone all soft and gravelly. Woody, too, is suddenly finding great interest in his boots.

"I just knew I had to make a change. All my life, I'd worked nine to five at the auto supply store, and I had some good years there, Mikey," he says, nodding toward a chipmunk-cheeked man stuffing a piece of birthday cake in his mouth. "But I needed to start over. I always liked cooking. Rita used to say I wore the apron in the family. So I thought, Why not? I needed the company bad. This place saved my life."

The room is suddenly very quiet. Miguel glances over at Tía Lola, who is wiping tears from her eyes. When she is done with her handkerchief, she hands it over to Mami, who dabs her eyes and passes it on to Carmen, who is blinking back tears. Miguel can't believe his rough-and-ready baseball coach would be so sappy. But then, Rudy is the first to say that a strong man shouldn't be afraid of his own feelings.

"Not only did I make it through those hard times,"

52

Rudy continues, "but I've had a heck of a good time. Only one thing hasn't been quite to my liking. . . ."

Rudy pauses for effect, but the twinkle in his eye suggests that whatever dissatisfaction he's going to confess won't be anything major. "I've never liked the name Rudy's." When a bunch of folks protest that they love the name, Rudy holds up his hands. "I've already decided. Listen up. I'm naming the place after you—that's right. You guys got me through, and that includes some new friends, now not so new." Rudy looks over at Mami and Tía Lola, who bow their heads modestly at the compliment they see coming.

"These two lovely ladies have taught me a bunch of recipes, and also a whole lot about friendship. So I thought Amigos Café would be a great name, to thank them and you and to remind us all of our warm southern neighbors, especially during these cold winter months!"

Everyone hoots and claps. After the noise dies down, old Colonel Charlebois bangs his cane on the floor to get everyone's attention.

"I would like to propose a toast!" he says, holding up his water glass. "To Rudy, who has created a gathering place for this town and given some of us who hadn't had a taste of home cooking in a long time the opportunity to eat well and gain back some lost pounds. But best of all has been the chance to renew old friendships and make some new ones. Hear! Hear!"

By the time the party is over, even Papi, who thought Mami was depriving his kids by moving them out of

New York City, is a convert. "I can see why you love this place," he admits as they walk to the car.

"It's a great place to live!" Carmen echoes.

"That's because we're with the people we love," Juanita speaks up. It's some old lesson Tía Lola once taught them.

"Except for Papi," Miguel reminds her.

His father reaches over and ruffles Miguel's hair fondly, stirring up a little halo of snowflakes. Appropriate for a boy whose middle name is Ángel.

●●●

The next morning, Papi shows up all by himself. "Let's just us three go for breakfast together. We'll swing by and pick up Carmen at the B&B on our way back. Sound good?"

Juanita is disappointed. "Why can't Carmen come, too?"

"Because it's just going to be our family, right, Papi?" Miguel looks up hopefully at his father. But instead of the fond smile of last night, Papi winces as if he's in pain.

"Families grow, families change," Papi says quietly. It sounds like another of Tía Lola's sayings.

And that's what he wants to talk about once they have sat down at the diner and the waitress has taken their order. They would have gone to Rudy's, but the restaurant will be closed for a whole week for a remodeling to go with the new name. Stargazer, who owns a local gift shop, and some of her artist friends will be painting murals on the inside walls—tropical jungle scenes that will make Señor Burro and Mr. Flamingo and the palm tree feel right at home. It was announced last night at the party.

"I learned a lot from being married to your mother," Papi begins. He is folding and refolding his napkin like it's some origami project the waitress gave him to do while he's waiting for his breakfast. "What can I say? We were kids when we got married. I, especially, had a lot of growing up to do. Too caught up with my own career as an artist, which wasn't getting off the ground. I was depressed. I admit I wasn't the best husband."

Oh boy, Miguel thinks. It's always worrisome when your parents take the long way down memory lane.

"Your mother made a lot of sacrifices. It was she who finished college and got her master's and held down a job so I could paint." The napkin has been folded down to such a tiny square, it might just disappear. Maybe it's not an origami project but a magic vanishing act, Miguel thinks, wishing he could vanish. He doesn't want to think about what's coming.

"It's really because of the mistakes I made that I'm sure I'll be a much better husband the second time around."

"So are you and Mami going to get married again?" Juanita asks excitedly. But suddenly, her face falls. "What about Carmen?"

Papi smiles in spite of himself.

"No, no, *mi'jita,*" Papi tells his little daughter. "Mami

55

and I— Our marriage, well, it's over. Sometimes we make mistakes and there's no going back to correct them. But we can learn from them and make better choices in the future."

"Like me losing the treasure hunt for my team but learning to pay attention," Juanita says, nodding.

"Exactly." Papi nods back, even though he can't know what Juanita is talking about. But Papi doesn't wait for an explanation. Soon the weekend will be over. He has some important news for them. "So, what I want to tell you is that I'm ready to be married."

A long silence follows this statement. Miguel attacks his own napkin, except instead of folding and refolding it, he is twisting it tight, wringing its neck.

"So, what do you kids think of Carmen?" Papi asks, like he's changing the subject to some totally unrelated question.

At least Juanita doesn't seem to catch on. "I love Carmen!" She says it so loud that some people turn in their booths to see what the little brown girl is so excited about.

"And you, *mi'jo*?" Papi asks delicately after waiting some seconds to hear what Miguel has to say.

But Miguel can't seem to find his tongue. He looks down at the napkin in his lap. He has managed to rip it apart, and has a piece in each hand.

"S'okay, *mi'jo*," Papi says. "I understand you need to get used to the idea. But it would mean a lot to me if you

56

could learn to love Carmen. She thinks the world of you, you know."

Miguel nods but keeps his head down. She thinks the world of the whole world, he wants to say. But he knows that would hurt his *papi*.

●●●

In the midafternoon, Papi and Carmen say their good-byes. Miguel gives Carmen a goodbye handshake, which she turns into a heartfelt hug.

"Hey, Miguel Ángel, thanks again for a wonderful visit!" she gushes.

"Thank you for coming," he says, glancing toward his *mami*.

"I wouldn't have missed it for the world!" Carmen gives him another hug.

"It was fun," Miguel concedes. It is hard to resist Carmen's enthusiasm.

At dinner, Mami queries them about "your breakfast meeting with your father." It bugs Miguel how his parents talk about each other like they themselves were never related. Your mother. Your father.

"He talked about learning from mistakes, like me not paying attention in class, but now I do," Juanita says, going on to give a garbled account of how Papi learned so much from being married to Mami.

"I'll say," Mami mutters. She doesn't like to criticize

their father in front of them, but sometimes she can't help herself.

"He said you're the greatest!" Juanita adds.

Mami replies with a *hmph,* then bites her lip to prevent any further criticism from coming out.

"Ay, querida," Tía Lola reminds her dear niece, "Daniel has grown up a lot. Remember, *los tropezones hacen levantar los pies!"*

"Stumbling might have taught him to pick up his feet, but meanwhile, what about the people he's stepped on along the way?"

Tía Lola must have a dozen sayings about forgiveness, but she says nothing. Sometimes you just have to let people express their hurt feelings. Mami would be the first to tell them that.

Mami folds her napkin and places it beside her uneaten plate of food. Then she hurries from the room, wiping her eyes on her sleeve since she doesn't have Tía Lola's handkerchief handy.

"Your *mami* will be just fine!" Tía Lola reassures them. "Those tears are just washing away the past so she can begin again, too."

"Did Papi really step on her, Tía Lola?" Juanita's bottom lip is quivering.

Tía Lola is shaking her head. "Let me put it this way: they both made the mistake of getting married too young. Afterward, they found out they disagreed on a whole bunch of things. But they would both agree on one thing: if they hadn't made that mistake, they would have missed out on having the two most wonderful kids! *No hay mal que por bien no venga.*"

Every bad thing has something good in it.

"Is that like 'Every cloud has a silver lining'?" Juanita wants to know.

Tía Lola looks surprised. "I had no idea that clouds had silver inside them." This must be science she never learned because she never went past fourth grade. So Miguel and Juanita have to explain. It's a saying, just like the ones she has been teaching them in Spanish.

"Don't you love sayings?" Tía Lola says after laughing at herself. "They really help you to remember wise things."

At the door, Mami has reappeared, her face shy with an apology. "Sorry, everybody. I just want you to know I made some mistakes, too."

"But you are picking up your feet, right, Mami?" Juanita says.

"And how," Mami says, kicking her heels up in the air just like Mr. Flamingo, now dangling from a ceiling hook at Amigos Café.

lesson six

En todas partes se cuecen habas
Everywhere, people cook beans

Now that Juanita is paying attention, she has made so many friends at school. Of course, it also doesn't hurt that Juanita is related to Tía Lola, whom everybody loves. It's just too bad that Juanita's birthday is in September, too early in the school year for her to have made a whole lot of friends. But now, midyear, could she ever throw the greatest party—even better than Rudy's!

Maybe she can have a half-year birthday party? But she isn't turning eight and a half until March. And it's now, in frigid February, that a birthday party would be most welcome.

"Tía Lola, what do you say I have an almost-eight-and-a-half-year-old birthday party?" Juanita proposes to her aunt as they are riding the bus to school on one of Tía Lola's teaching days.

"I think it's a wonderful idea! We need a party every week in this kind of weather."

Juanita gazes up lovingly at her aunt. The wonderful thing about Tía Lola is that she thinks like a kid, but being a grown-up, she can actually make wishes come true.

"So when should we have the party?" her aunt asks. "When you turn eight and a half or now?"

Juanita doesn't have to think about it. "Now!"

Tía Lola laughs in total agreement. *"No dejes para mañana lo que puedas hacer hoy."*

"We have the same saying in English! 'Don't leave for tomorrow what you can do today.' " Juanita is so excited when English and Spanish actually match. Usually they don't because each language is like a fingerprint, totally unique.

"The Americans must have copied us!" Tía Lola says, not doubting for a second that Spanish speakers think of everything first.

"But, Tía Lola, how can you be sure?"

"Un pajarito me lo dijo." Tía Lola winks playfully.

"We also have that saying! 'A little bird told me.' " Juanita is amazed. It's like when a baby discovers that the hands at the ends of her arms belong to her and she can move them all by herself. "That one you copied from us,

61

right?" Juanita teases back. It's a game now: What came first, the Spanish saying or the English one?

"I think we both copied it from the little birds," Tía Lola remarks, laughing. "By the way, I haven't seen a bird in a long time."

"Tía Lola!" Juanita narrows her eyes. She isn't sure whether her aunt is still teasing her. "You do know that most birds go south in the winter, right?" She watches her aunt's face, trying to figure out if Tía Lola already knows this.

But Tía Lola's face is hard to read. "I guess those little birds forgot to tell me before they left!" Just when Juanita is convinced that her aunt missed out on basic science by not going past fourth grade, Tía Lola winks. "Maybe they were chirping in English and I didn't understand?"

It's Mami who vetoes the half-birthday-party idea. "I don't mind a party party," she explains. "But if you call it a birthday party, people will feel they have to bring a gift."

Exactly, Juanita thinks.

"And if everyone in the world starts having half birthday parties as well as full birthday parties, we'll never save enough money to buy a house."

Juanita loves the idea that they might someday actually have their very own house. But she also hates the idea of moving out of this wonderful old one, with so many nooks and crannies, and an attic with a little bedroom for Tía Lola, and a long staircase with a sliding banister, and a big bay window at the landing. "Does Colonel Charlebois want this one back?"

"No, he still wants to keep renting to us. It just makes more economic sense for us to buy rather than rent," Mami explains unhelpfully. When Mami or Papi starts talking about mortgages or income taxes, Juanita is just glad she can wait until she's older to find out about all that stuff.

"Okay." Juanita lets out a long sigh. "I suppose my half birthday will go by just like any other stupid day. . . ." As she heads out of the room, her little shoulders droop with the burden of not getting her way.

●●●

Upstairs, she delivers the news to Tía Lola, who instantly puts on her magic thinking cap. It's not a real cap, just a look on her face where you can almost see grand thoughts parading across her forehead.

"Let's see . . . what other kind of party can we throw in *febrero*? I know a good one for the end of February! We can celebrate *carnaval*!"

"What's that?" Juanita doesn't feel too hopeful if it's some holiday she has never heard of. She herself was thinking of Valentine's Day.

"You've never heard of *carnaval*? All the more reason to have a party, then! *Carnaval* is huge back home. It's a big celebration right before Lent."

"What's Lent?" Juanita wants to know.

Tía Lola looks at her niece in total disbelief. "Your parents *were* young not to teach you these things! *Bueno,* Tía Lola will! *Más vale tarde que nunca.*"

Before Juanita can tell her aunt that "Better late than never" is also a saying in English, Tía Lola winks. "Don't tell me! You have the same one in English, too. And I know you didn't copy it from us or we from you. It's because we're all one human family, even if we speak different languages and come from different countries. Like the saying says: *En todas partes se cuecen habas.*"

Everywhere, people cook beans? "That's one I never heard before in English, Tía Lola," Juanita admits. "What does it mean?"

"There are certain things that people everywhere in the world do, like cook beans or have babies or dream dreams or fall in love."

"Or want birthday parties," Juanita joins in dreamily, "and half birthday parties and lots and lots of wonderful presents. . . ." Juanita imagines a Chinese girl and an African girl and a French girl and a Mexican girl, all wishing for a birthday party with lots and lots of gifts. . . .

The thought of a Mexican girl reminds Juanita of Ofie. Last week, Ms. Sweeney's room had a sharing circle about birthdays. When it was her turn, Ofie told the class that she had never had a birthday party because she can't have friends over on account of her parents being Mexicans.

What in the world does having Mexican parents have to do with not having friends over? Juanita wondered.

She would have asked, but Milton's hand had already shot up. This time, however, Ms. Sweeney did not pause for questions. In fact, she hurried on to somebody else's birthday story.

Thinking back now on Ofie's story, Juanita feels lucky. Not only can she have friends over for sleepovers and playdates, but she has had a birthday party with gifts once a year all her life, for as long as she can remember.

"Do Mexicans celebrate *carnaval,* Tía Lola?" Juanita wants to know.

"Why, of course!" Tía Lola says. "Why do you ask?"

So Juanita explains about Ofie never having had a birthday party in her life. "So if we have *carnaval,* Ofie'll get to celebrate a holiday her family would have celebrated back in Mexico."

Now it's Tía Lola who is gazing lovingly at her niece. "You are an angel, you know that?"

"No, I'm not, Tía Lola. Miguel is the Ángel!" Juanita grins. She is proud of herself for thinking of this little joke.

But Tía Lola keeps shaking her head as if to say, I know an angel when I see one, even if her name is Juana Inés.

●●●

Mrs. Stevens thinks the idea of a school-wide *carnaval* celebration is *fantástico.* Every year, Bridgeport Elementary has a talent show or a candy sale to raise money for field trips. So this year, let it be a *carnaval*. A great way to complement the Spanish lessons Tía Lola has been giving.

Soon the whole school is learning all about *carnaval* in Spanish class. How it comes right before Lent, a time of year when you give up fun stuff and fast, which means you don't pig out on anything and you think about how to be a better person. But right before the start of this thoughtful time of year, you have one last celebration, called *carnaval,* in which you eat lots of yummy food and party and dance and have tons of fun. And the best part is that everyone dresses up in a costume, which is cool, like having another Halloween in the middle of winter!

Milton raises his hand. "Can we use our Halloween costumes?"

"Of course you can," Ms. Sweeney says. She must see some worry flash across Ofie's face, because she adds, "But you don't have to dress up if you don't want to. Am I right, Tía Lola?"

Tía Lola nods vigorously. "The point is to have a party. Everybody in the world loves a party!" The class claps wildly, proving Tía Lola right. *"En todas partes se cuecen habas,"* she adds, but even Milton is too excited to ask Juanita for a translation.

Yes, Juanita is thinking, everywhere in the world people love to party. It's kind of nice to have something happy the whole world can share—besides beans, which, Juanita hates to tell her aunt, are not among her favorite things.

"I've been thinking about your little friend Ofie," Tía Lola says to Juanita on their ride home on the bus. They've already gone by the farm where Ofie gets off with her older sister, María, and the farmer's son, Tyler. "You said her birthday was in August?"

Juanita nods. Ms. Sweeney wrote everyone's birth date on the big calendar, but since Ofie's was in the summer, Juanita didn't pay that much attention. "I think it was like the last week in August."

"That means her half birthday is in late February, which is about the same time as *carnaval,* so what I was thinking—"

"That's a great idea!" Juanita interrupts Tía Lola. It's as if Juanita were a mind reader, because she knows exactly what her aunt was about to suggest. Why not make the *carnaval* fiesta also be Ofie's half birthday party?! And since the celebration is at school, Ofie doesn't have to worry about having friends over.

But there is only one other problem. Mami has vetoed the idea of half birthdays. If you do it for one kid, every kid in the world will want one.

"I have a feeling your mother will make an exception in this case," Tía Lola says. *"Toda regla tiene su excepción."*

"I know," Juanita says. "We have that saying, too." There is an exception to every rule, in Spanish, in English—in fact, everywhere in the world.

●●●

A day later, when Tía Lola boards the bus with Juanita, they sit across the aisle from Ofie and her big sister, María. "So what would you like to dress up as for *carnaval?*" Tía Lola asks the girls.

The sisters exchange a glance. "We don't have costumes," Ofie speaks up. "We're not allowed to dress up for Halloween or beg for treats. We have to come straight home after school."

"Those are the rules, I know," Tía Lola says. "But we're talking about wishes."

The girls' faces soften. They, too, love this special aunt. All their own *tías* are back in Mexico, Ofie has told Juanita.

"I would be a princess," the older one, María, says shyly, then looks down, embarrassed.

"I would be a princess, too," Ofie says, "or a mermaid."

"Wonderful choices." Tía Lola smiles approvingly.

"I was a princess last Halloween and a mermaid the year before that," Juanita pipes up. "You guys want to wear my old costumes for the *carnaval* at school?"

The girls' faces light up. "Really?" Ofie asks in an awed whisper.

"I don't think they'll fit us." María is older, more doubtful. But her face betrays such longing, Juanita would hate to disappoint her.

"I can alter them, no problem," Tía Lola explains. "I worked many, many years as a seamstress." In fact, last summer she sewed all the uniforms for Miguel's baseball team.

"Can we really borrow them?" Ofie says, her eyes sparkling with excitement.

It's only now that Juanita realizes she has left herself high and dry. Unless her mother buys her a new costume—and Mami is saving for a new house—Juanita will have nothing to wear for *carnaval* herself. But seeing these two sisters so happy makes her reckless. For a moment, she understands how fairy godmothers must feel all the time.

"So what are you going to wear as *your* costume?" Miguel asks Juanita after the girls have gotten off the bus. He'll probably just dress as Big Papi in his number 34 Red Sox jersey.

"Whatever," Juanita says, shrugging. "Costumes aren't required for *carnaval,* right, Tía Lola?"

Her aunt nods slowly. "You don't need a costume. You need a new name: Juanita Inés de los Ángeles." Juanita Inés of the Angels.

●●●

The first *carnaval* at Bridgeport Elementary will be talked about for years to come.

The school's hallways are transformed with garlands of brightly colored *papel picado;* the walls are covered with paintings of palm trees and parrots and humongous flowers as big as a kindergartener. Rudy and Tía Lola

69

have cooked up a storm in the kitchen. In the lunchroom, the tables line the walls, leaving an open area in the center. Each grade parades in, showing off their costumes—superheroes and pirates and baseball players and princesses and witches—blowing whistles and recorders, beating drums and tambourines, while families and friends hoot and holler and clap. It's pandemonium, as Mrs. Stevens calls it—the fun kind.

Once everyone sits down to eat, Mr. Bicknell, the sixth-grade teacher, who also gives music lessons, blows a few notes on his trumpet. Lo and behold, out of the kitchen comes an angel carrying a birthday cake and heading straight for the table where a little Mexican mermaid is sitting with other second graders. Suddenly, Mr. Bicknell begins to blow "Happy Birthday," and all the teachers and students and, of course, the angel join in, singing, "Happy half birthday to you."

"*Feliz medio cumpleaños,* Ofie," Tía Lola sings from her post by the kitchen door.

Everyone watches the little mermaid. At first she seems unsure, as if she is debating whether to confess it's not really her birthday. But suddenly, they can see Ofie's relief as she realizes this *is* her half birthday. Her face is luminous with happiness.

Having completed her mission, the angel returns to stand by Tía Lola. "That was so fun!" Juanita confesses to her aunt. "Did you see how surprised Ofie was? Thanks for letting me carry the cake."

"It was you who thought of half birthday parties," Tía

Lola reminds her niece. "You who contributed your old costumes. Who else should have carried the cake?"

You, Juanita is thinking. After all, it was Tía Lola who organized this amazing *carnaval* celebration in a little over two weeks. Not only that, she made sure every kid had a costume to wear . . . including her niece. Yes, earlier this evening Juanita had come sliding down the banister in her school clothes. She was trying to be upbeat and cheerful, but truthfully, she was feeling a little sorry for herself. She was going to her first *carnaval* party ever, and she didn't have a costume to wear.

But there, hanging like a piñata from a plant hook in the living room, was the most beautiful angel costume! Tía Lola had sewn the gown from some old satin sheets, adding glittery trim to the collar and sleeves and weaving a sparkling halo out of the same trim. Then, from the papier-mâché for her piñatas, Tía Lola had fashioned two awesome wings.

Juanita had gasped. This was an outfit fit for a real angel!

"I told you that you are an angel," Tía Lola whispered as she helped Juanita dress.

Now, gazing out at the lunchroom, Juanita smiles. Everyone looks so happy! Every kid seems to be celebrating a birthday or a half birthday or a quarter birthday. Every grown-up seems delighted to be allowed a night of childhood magic. Tía Lola was absolutely right, Juanita is thinking: Everywhere in the world, people cook beans and love parties and deserve to be happy. Juanita might not be an angel, but this *is* heaven.

lesson seven

Quien tiene boca llega a Roma
If you have a mouth, you can get to Rome

Miguel wakes up, feeling excited and happy before he even remembers why. Today is the first day of winter recess, and he and Juanita and Tía Lola are headed for New York City. Mami will drive them up to Burlington to catch a midmorning bus to the Port Authority Bus Terminal. Papi will be waiting for them there, probably with Carmen hooked to his arm.

A little cloud sails into his thoughts, staining the clear blue sky of Miguel's happiness. He still can't get used to Carmen *always* being along.

But that cloud soon dissipates. Carmen can sometimes think up fun things. A few days ago, a package arrived. Inside, they found a Knicks sweatshirt and a card saying *Prepare yourself, Miguel Ángel, we're going to Madison Square Garden with José and his dad to see a game!* And in that same package, they also found a ballerina tote bag and a note saying *Juana Inés, guess what? I got you and Tía Lola and me and Ming tickets to a matinee of the New York City Ballet!* Even Tía Lola got something—two pretty handkerchiefs, monogrammed with a big loopy *L. May these catch only happy tears.* Tía Lola read the note out loud, her eyes moistening with happy tears. *"¡Qué muchacha tan cariñosa!"* What a sweet girl!

"I don't see why she's sending presents. She's going to be seeing you guys in a week," Mami commented.

"You catch more flies with a drop of honey than with a quart of vinegar, that's why," Tía Lola noted. "She's just trying to be nice, Linda."

"She might be trying a little too hard," Mami had said in a voice that was trying hard not to sound critical. Maybe Mami was just miffed that she herself hadn't gotten a gift in the package from Carmen.

But Mami had received a thank-you card, which she read carefully. What was Mami thinking? Miguel wondered, studying his mother's face as she read. He wished he could know, without asking, whether it was okay for him to begin to like Carmen.

Now, as he dresses and thinks about Mami staying all

73

alone for the coming week, Miguel feels a pang. This is ridiculous, he thinks. He hasn't even left home and he's already homesick! He'll call Mami every day, maybe even send her a couple of postcards. But he's determined to have a great time seeing his *papi* and grandparents and going to that Knicks game with his best friend, José. "YES!!!" He pumps his arm in a show of resolve. "Yes, yes, yes!"

That's when Miguel notices that he has lost his voice. Oh no! If Mami finds out, she is not going to let him go to New York City. Never mind that Miguel doesn't have a sore throat or feel feverish or anything.

All thoughts of homesickness have vanished from Miguel's mind. Somehow he has to get on that bus with Tía Lola and Juanita without Mami catching on that he has laryngitis.

❋❋❋

Miguel rolls his suitcase out to the upstairs hallway. Down in the kitchen, he can hear voices—Tía Lola's, Mami's. Juanita must be in the bathroom, door closed, water running.

He raps lightly. "Juanita!" But his voice is a mere whisper. He raps again.

"Who's there?"

Miguel whispers his name, but of course his sister can't hear him. He knocks harder.

Juanita yanks open the door, her soapy face

74

looking annoyed. "I'm using the bathroom," she explains unnecessarily.

"I need your help, Nita," Miguel whispers. He looks over his shoulder, checking to see if someone's coming up the stairs.

"What's wrong?" Juanita is suddenly more curious than she is annoyed. Her soapy face is forgotten. "Why are you whispering?"

"I've lost my voice. But it's not a cold," Miguel is quick to explain.

"Maybe you're just going through pooberty, you think?" Juanita suggests. "We learned about it in science— how boys' voices change when they start getting older and going through pooberty."

Maybe it's because Juanita's standing in the bathroom, but Miguel does not like some stage of life he is soon to enter being called pooberty. However, this is no time to argue with his little sister and risk a scene that might land him in bed with a thermometer in his mouth. "It's not puberty, Juanita, it's just laryngitis. But you've got to help me, okay? Otherwise, Mami will cancel our trip!"

Juanita's eyes widen at this terrible possibility. Thankfully, she doesn't think of the alternative: that Mami might let *her* go to New York with their aunt but without her big brother. At moments like this, Miguel feels a rush of tenderness for his innocent little sister, who can be so easily tricked.

"We'll go down to the kitchen together. You do all the talking at breakfast, okay?"

75

Juanita nods solemnly, as if she has been assigned some near-impossible task, when actually—and Miguel isn't going to say this—Juanita usually does most of the talking anyhow.

●●●

In the kitchen, Mami and Tía Lola are sitting at the table, gossiping. Each one is holding a mug of coffee with both hands, like that's going to keep them warm this cold winter morning.

The minute Juanita and Miguel enter, the conversation stops. Mami and Tía Lola must have been talking about something the kids aren't meant to hear. Now, with the topic off-limits, they unfortunately focus all their attention on the two children entering the kitchen, one of whom is trying hard to make himself inconspicuous.

"Hey, sleepyheads!" Mami teases. "Are you packed up and ready to go?"

Juanita jumps in a little too eagerly. "Our suitcases are out in the hall already. Miguel carried them both down. He's so *healthy* and strong!"

Miguel wishes he could kick his little sister under the table. But how can he when they are standing shoulder to shoulder? The overkill about his health will tip Mami off.

"He sure is! Healthy and strong, and handsome, too!"

Mami beams Miguel a radiant smile of mother love. "Come give Mami a kiss," she commands, stretching out her arms to him.

Miguel doesn't like it when his *mami* treats him like a little boy. But he's not about to make a point of being grown-up when he has to be as speechless as a baby. He shuffles over and plants a semi-reluctant kiss on Mami's cheek. But before he can move away, she pulls him back for another.

"Are you going to miss me?" She looks up at him, her eyes playful but a little sad, anticipating his departure.

Miguel nods and keeps his own head down, afraid his eyes will betray him. Luckily, his mother thinks Miguel is overcome with emotion and can't answer.

"How about me?" Juanita asks petulantly. "How come you don't ask me if *I'm* going to miss you?" What a time for his little sister to get jealous! But it ends up being a lucky thing, because now Mami bends over backward to focus on Juanita.

Meanwhile, Miguel plows through his bowl of cereal, not looking up once. He's afraid to make eye contact with Mami and risk inviting conversation.

"You are a quiet boy this morning," Tía Lola observes as Miguel clears his empty bowl from the table.

"The cat got his tongue," Mami teases.

Horrified, Tía Lola rushes over and forces Miguel's mouth open. Relief shows on her face. "His tongue is fine! But his throat looks a little red. Are you feeling

77

okay?" she asks, planting a cool hand on Miguel's warm forehead.

Thankfully, Juanita is back on track, remembering their plan of action. " 'Cat got your tongue' just means someone is being quiet," she explains to their aunt.

"I see," Tía Lola says, looking thoughtfully at Miguel.

When Mami goes out to the driveway to warm up the car, Miguel and Juanita rush to their aunt's side. "Please, Tía Lola, help us!" They explain what is going on.

"I really want to go see Papi," Miguel adds in his raspy voice.

"But if you're sick . . . I don't know." Tía Lola looks torn. She wants to take good care of her nephew, but she also doesn't want to disappoint him.

"I'm not sick at all, Tía Lola, I promise," Miguel says desperately.

"But your throat did look a little red. Let me check again."

Just then, Mami walks in the door, which leaves Tía Lola with no alternative. She can't examine her nephew's throat or she will give his secret away.

"I suppose you can rest up at your father's if you are catching a little cold," Tía Lola whispers as she and her niece and nephew are putting on their coats.

"I am *not* catching a cold," Miguel whispers back.

"What's all the whispering about?" Mami wants to know, joining them in the mudroom. She looks suspiciously from one startled face to another.

Juanita comes to the rescue again. "We just have a

favor to ask you, Mami. Can we listen to *Harry Potter* on the way up to Burlington?" Mami has checked out the latest book in the series from the library.

As they ride in silence, listening to the audiobook, Miguel is struck by this brilliant move on his sister's part. If the CD were not playing, Mami would be peppering the backseat with nervous questions about their trip.

When they are almost at the station, Mami turns the CD player off. She begins coaching them on how to make the bus transfers, what to do if one of them gets separated or lost. No doubt she is remembering their first trip to New York City with Tía Lola. Their aunt had gotten lost, and for several nerve-racking hours they had not been able to find her.

"No te preocupes," Tía Lola assures her. Mami is not to worry. *"El que tiene boca llega a Roma."*

If you have a mouth, you can get to Rome? "But we're not going to Rome, Tía Lola." Juanita looks baffled. "We're going to New York City, remember?"

"It's an expression in Spanish, Nita," Mami explains. "It means if you can talk, you can find your way anywhere. The reason Rome was chosen . . ." Mami drones on about the olden days, how the Spaniards ruled the world and the center of their Catholic religion was Rome.

Miguel is relieved. When grown-ups get educational, they spare you having to talk. He closes his eyes, relaxed at last. That's when he notices a slight, insignificant soreness at the back of his throat.

It's nothing, he thinks, dismissing it. But by the time

they arrive in New York City that evening and meet Papi and Carmen, Miguel is flagging. His throat is definitely sore.

Tía Lola is upset with herself. "I should never have let you come."

"Tía Lola, it's no use crying over spilled milk!" Juanita reminds her aunt.

"What spilled milk?" Tía Lola looks around the floor of the big, crowded station. "I didn't spill milk."

"Don't worry, Tía Lola," Carmen says, putting her arm around Miguel. "We'll give him tons of TLC here!"

Tía Lola wrinkles her nose. "TLC?" She must think it's some sort of cough syrup, because she shakes her head. "I have my own recipe, a mint tea of *yerbabuena* with honey and cinnamon and cloves."

Oh brother! Miguel suddenly wishes that he were back home, tucked in his bed, with no one to bother him. When you aren't feeling well, it's hard to be patient with explanations or to get tender loving care from a stranger, even if she *is* destined to be your stepmother.

●●●

All week long, Miguel stays home in Papi's apartment. The first few days, he doesn't mind at all because he feels miserable. On Tuesday night, his temperature spikes so high that even Papi, who usually believes that the best way to treat a fever is to give it the cold shoulder, wants to take him to the hospital. But by Friday, Miguel feels totally recovered. The only fever he has is cabin fever! Man, he can't wait to get out of this apartment. Good thing the Knicks game is tonight. It'll be the one fun thing he gets to do before they have to head home early Sunday. Miguel is going to make tonight's outing count for a whole week of lost vacation time!

But when Mami calls that morning before going to work, his bigmouthed little sister blabs that Miguel still had a fever last night.

"Mami, it wasn't a real fever," Miguel argues. "It was only ninety-nine."

But Mami has made up her mind. "I'm sorry, Miguelito. I know it means a lot to you. But you're still weak, and this game is at night and it's winter. . . . It's for your own good," she adds. The old excuse.

"But it's the Knicks game," Miguel protests. His voice is back, but it might as well be gone. His *mami* refuses to listen. "I've been in bed all week! I'm sick of being sick." Miguel keeps pleading, but sometimes you can just tell when a parent is not going to budge.

When he gets off the phone, Miguel is ready to kill his little sister. But Juanita is already feeling horrible. "I'm sorry, I'm sorry," she keeps blubbering, like that's going to change anything.

There's only one person with the power to turn things around. "Please, Papi, can't you just take me?" Miguel asks.

81

Papi shakes his head sadly. "It'd just cause trouble, believe me. Like your Tía Lola says— How does that saying go, Tía Lola, about the soldier and the captain?"

"Donde manda capitán, no manda soldado."

"That's right." Papi nods. "Where the captain is in charge, the soldier can't give orders. Your *mami* is the boss."

"But, Papi, you're the boss, too!"

"Try telling that to your *mami*," Papi mutters.

"We can watch the game on TV," Juanita offers. "You can have all my turns, okay?" Usually, she and Miguel alternate who gets to watch what program.

Miguel knows his little sister is trying to make it up to him. But Juanita doesn't get it *again*. Watching a game on TV in a small apartment with your family is not the same as being at the actual live game in a huge arena with your best friend and other fans, cheering on your home team!

Only Carmen seems to understand. She looks at Miguel with sad eyes, as if she wishes she could defy captains and soldiers and whisk her future stepson away to watch the Knicks play the Bulls at Madison Square Garden.

Miguel tries a new tack. "Carmen'll lose all that money she paid for our tickets." Maybe championing his girlfriend's pocketbook will make Papi change his mind?

But his father has already thought up a solution. "I'll call José's dad and explain. He and José can go to the game and scalp our tickets. We'll probably make enough money on our five to cover the cost of all seven tickets. Next time you come down, *mi'jo*, I promise you—"

But Miguel has already rolled over in bed and pulled his blanket over his head. Who cares about seeing a game months from now? He has had it with his family! As he lies there under his covers, he begins plotting his escape. He is going to make it to Madison Square Garden to see the game no matter what Captain Mami or Officer Papi have to say. After all, Miguel is not in the military, so why does he have to obey?

Later that morning, Papi takes Tía Lola and Juanita to lunch over at Abuelito's and Abuelita's. Miguel would love to see his grandparents, but Abuelita's health is fragile. She has had one cold after another this winter. It's probably best not to take any chances by bringing Miguel along, in case he is still contagious.

"I don't know about leaving you alone." Papi worries. He has taken most of the week off from his day job, window-dressing department stores, to be with his children and their aunt. Although Papi isn't usually that protective, he is still unsure about his new neighborhood. It was only January when he moved to Brooklyn to be closer to his parents and to Carmen. Recently, there have been a few incidents—roaming teens vandalizing properties and shoplifting from local stores. Not big-time serious gangs, but still.

Miguel would just as soon stay alone in the apartment, especially given his plan to take off to Madison Square Garden once everyone is gone. He doesn't know how to get there from Brooklyn, but he's sure he can find out by asking. What was that saying his aunt told them in the car about going to Rome? Once there, he'll find José and José's *papi* and go in with them. The other four tickets they can sell.

But just his luck: Carmen offers to take off at lunchtime from her job as a lawyer in a law firm to stay with Miguel. "I'm fine," he keeps saying, but he is going to lose his voice all over again, protesting his good health.

Just before they depart, Papi calls Carmen. She's leaving the office right now, catching the subway. Papi and Tía Lola and Juanita can go ahead to lunch, as she'll be there in less than twenty minutes.

Finally, with one last round of Papi's admonitions to lock and chain the door, not to open it to anyone except Carmen, to look in the peephole first, Papi and Tía Lola and Juanita depart. Miguel watches them as they come out the front door of the building, cross the street, and then turn at the corner and disappear. Quickly, he gets out of bed and puts on his clothes. As he is pulling on his Knicks sweatshirt, he feels a pang. Carmen is going to come back to the apartment and go crazy over his absence. Still, Miguel can't let himself think about that. It's their fault for being overly protective. He's been housebound now for five days, and soon winter recess will be over and he'll have spent his whole vacation in bed.

Besides, he is leaving a note. He addresses it to *Papi &
Tía Lola & Juanita,* and only as an afterthought adds *&
Carmen.*

> Please don't worry!!! I'm meet-
> ing José and his father at the
> game. I'll be back as soon as
> it's over.   Miguel

He props the paper on his pillow and feels his heart
beating hard. This is really his first major act of disobe-
dience, and he knows he will probably get in big trouble. But just the thought of his parents' unfairness in
denying him one single fun thing on his vacation puts
him back on track. He strides out, turning only to check
that the door is securely locked.

● ● ●

Once on the chilly street, Miguel stops a man in a leather
jacket and asks him, "Which way to Madison Square
Garden?" The man shrugs. Either he doesn't know or he
doesn't understand English.

The next person he stops is an elderly woman walking a tiny dog and carrying a little bag and scooper.
Someone that careful and tidy must know directions
really well.

"Madison Square Garden?" she repeats, narrowing

her eyes as if she might see the complex from here in Brooklyn. "Let's see. Madison Square Garden . . . ," she says again. "Madison Square Garden." Perhaps she thinks that the more she repeats the name, the more likely she is to remember where it is. "What are you going to do at Madison Square Garden by yourself, young man?" she finally asks, sounding irritated, as if she'll only make the effort to remember directions if Miguel can give her a good enough reason why he wants to go there.

So much for Tía Lola's saying that if you have a mouth, you can get to Rome. Miguel can't even get to Manhattan from Brooklyn!

He might as well start walking until he finds a subway station. Otherwise, Miguel is going to be standing in front of his father's apartment building when Carmen arrives.

But once he finds the familiar sign and descends, he discovers that the token booth is empty. A notice at the window directs customers to buy MetroCards at the machine. If he wants directions, he'd best head back up and try his luck at one of the little shops that line the street.

As he bolts up the stairs, he smacks right into someone coming down. Miguel is about to apologize, but the next thing he knows, he has been slammed against the wall.

"Watch where you're going, brown boy!" A tough-looking guy, as brown as Miguel, is glaring down at him.

"I didn't see you," Miguel tries explaining.

"YOU DIDN'T SEE ME?!" the guy screams in

his face. It's now that Miguel notices that this guy has a whole group of his friends with him. But he is the toughest-looking of the bunch, though they all look tough enough, dressed in black with body piercings in places that look painful: nostrils, eyebrows, studs along the rims of their ears. "Whatcha mean, you didn't see me?"

Miguel feels his heart beating so strong that he's afraid this mean guy will tell him to shut the thing up.

"Come on, Rafi!" the girl clinging to his arm pleads. "Leave him alone. He's just a little kid."

Normally, Miguel would take offense at this description of himself. After all, in four weeks, he'll be eleven years old. But he'd just as soon have this tough think he's Juanita's age if that would make him leave Miguel alone.

But the guy seems annoyed, being told what to do by his girlfriend. He gives Miguel another shove. "Kid? He's no kid! How old are you, anyhow?" he growls.

Miguel is sure that whatever he says, it will be the wrong answer. Besides, he can't seem to find his voice. It's as if his laryngitis has come back, big-time.

"Rafi, come on, the train's coming. . . ." The girlfriend yanks at Rafi's arm. And sure enough, a train is rushing into the station with a deafening roar. But Rafi seems undecided whether to follow his girlfriend and buddies, who are ducking under the turnstile, or, like a cat with a mouse, keep playing with his terrified quarry.

Just then the doors of the train whoosh open. Out of the corner of his eye, Miguel catches two sights that make

87

his heart soar. The first is a pair of uniformed policemen disembarking, and right behind them, a face he never thought he would be so happy to see—Carmen's!

It takes her only a second to size up the situation. When she does, she springs into action, a lioness defending her cub. "GET AWAY FROM HIM!" she screams as she dashes through the turnstile, pulling something out of her bag. It's the little canister of pepper spray she was showing off to Tía Lola the other night.

But by the time she is ready to use the spray and Rafi has turned around to punch out whoever is telling him what to do, it's too late. The policemen have tackled him: one has him in a neck hold, the other is clamping handcuffs on him. Meanwhile, Rafi is screaming foul language the likes of which Miguel has never heard before.

By now, Carmen has raced to Miguel's side to shield him from the kicks the panicked Rafi is throwing in the air. Over her shoulder, Miguel catches a last glimpse of the faces of the other gang members. Their mouths have dropped open—none of them looks so tough anymore; the girlfriend is crying black-mascara tears. The doors close. The train pulls out of the station, carrying them safely away from their vanquished leader.

On the walk back to the apartment, Carmen slips her arm around Miguel, as if to protect him from any further thugs. She is unusually quiet. Probably she is still shaken, and more than a little angry at him. Miguel doesn't blame her one bit. He wants to apologize, but the cat really has got his tongue. He can't think of where to begin. Besides, he is waiting for the scolding he knows he has coming to him.

He has to admit, Carmen was so brave, the way she threw herself in harm's way to protect him. She also didn't get him in trouble with the policemen by disclosing that Miguel had no business being outside of his father's apartment by himself. In fact, she had refused to press charges, saying that Rafi was just a kid who needed help. He probably didn't have a nice family like Miguel's to take care of him.

"Thank you," Miguel finally says after several minutes of silence. "You were awesome. I'm sorry."

Instead of lecturing him, she squeezes his arm. "If anything should happen to you, Miguel Ángel, I just . . ." She falls silent again, as if the worst thing that could happen to her would be if something happened to him.

She hasn't even asked, but Miguel knows he owes her an explanation. So he tells her: how much he really appreciated the tickets she'd gotten; how he didn't want to miss the game; how he wanted to see his best friend, José; how he did leave a note. Even so, he knows he made a wrong decision and was being totally selfish. Papi and Tía Lola and Juanita would have been worried to death about him.

"And Carmen, too," she reminds him.

"I'll never do something stupid like that again, promise."

"Or at least tell me first, so I can run away with you next time!" Carmen is grinning when Miguel looks up at her.

"Come on," she says. "I'm going to call your *mami* and talk to her. She's probably just worried because she's far away. If she agrees, we'll tear up your note and write a new one, telling your *papi* and Tía Lola and Juanita to meet us at Madison Square Garden. I'll call José's dad so he knows not to scalp our tickets. It's worth trying, don't you think?"

Miguel can't help but grin back. The way he's feeling right now, even if they end up watching the game on TV, he'll have a good time. Carmen will think of some way to make it fun. And if they do go, Miguel will be relieved of having to ask directions, because Carmen probably knows how to get to Madison Square Garden, as well as Rome, on her very own.

lesson eight

Nunca es tarde cuando la dicha es buena
It's never too late when you're in luck
(or something like that)

Back in Vermont, winter drags on. The one bright spot is Miguel's eleventh birthday at the end of March, but in twenty-four hours it's gone!

Then April begins, with one small step toward spring, four giant steps back into cold weather. The town grows grayer, the people paler. The few out on the streets move with slow steps so as not to slip on the icy sidewalks. The pace is so sluggish, the whole state could be in hibernation.

But Rudy's Amigos Café is rocking, the one lively, tropical spot for miles around. Every Wednesday it's Spanish night, with the whole menu printed *en español*. Tía Lola helps with the cooking. She comes out of the kitchen with her big pot of tasty food, piling on seconds (for free). Afterward, the tables are pushed back and Tía Lola offers dancing lessons—salsa and merengue and *cha-cha-cha*—to work off all those extra servings nobody can resist.

Between her school lessons and her restaurant lessons, Tía Lola is being kept *muy, muy ocupada*. Anyone in town can tell you what that means: very, very busy. In fact, the whole county is slowly becoming bilingual.

"Tía Lola, not only did you learn to teach in school, you've learned to teach everywhere!" Juanita exclaims as she and her aunt ride to the bus to Bridgeport Elementary on a wintry morning—too cold for April, for heaven's sake.

Tía Lola smiles happily. "I have been so lucky," she admits, shaking her head in disbelief. "I thought I would come to Vermont and be so lonely and sick for home. Instead, I am having the most fun I ever had in my whole life. I've seen *Nueva* York, and a ballet, and even a Kicky game!"

"Knicks, Tía Lola," Miguel calls from the back of the bus, where he's sitting with Dean and Sam. His friends have heard all about his adventures in New York City, including his near-mugging in the subway. Of course,

Miguel has used the imagination fifth graders are known for and touched up the incident, so it's him jumping the turnstile, pulling out the pepper spray, with Rafi's girl-friend pleading at his feet, "Please spare my boyfriend, please!"

But one part of the story that Miguel hasn't had to improve is how Carmen managed to convince Mami to let him go to the Knicks game. Not only that, Carmen and Mami have had several conversations since then. Miguel can tell that his *mami* now really and truly wants him and Juanita to get along with Carmen. In fact, Mami has admitted that the children's father is lucky to have found a woman like Carmen to keep his feet on the ground. "Better her than me," she has added, less generously.

Tía Lola tries again. "Okay, okay, a Kee-nee-kee game!" But no matter how much you coach her, Tía Lola just can't pronounce certain words in English. "I have been so lucky coming to Vermont, learning to teach at your school, making so many new *amigos: el* Rudy, *la señora* Stevens, *la* Mrs. Prouty, *la jovencita* Sweeney . . ." Tía Lola starts to count them, but suddenly, she stops. Nervously, she touches her forehead, her chest, her left shoulder, then her right, finally kissing her thumb.

"What in the world are you doing, Tía Lola?" Juanita asks, mystified.

"Just making the sign of the cross. To protect myself. It's bad luck to boast about being lucky."

"But why?" Juanita is looking at Tía Lola like she just dropped in from outer space, not the Dominican Republic.

"It's one of our *costumbres,* you know—a custom from the old country, like our sayings," Tía Lola explains.

Juanita starts thinking back to when she might have boasted recently. But nothing bad happened after she came back from winter recess bragging about going to see the New York City Ballet with Ming and Carmen and Tía Lola. In fact, except for winter dragging on, her life is wonderful! At school, she has a really nice teacher and so many friends. And now that she pays attention in class, every day is an adventure.

"But there have been many, many, many unlucky things, too," Tía Lola says loudly, as if she wants to make sure that whoever might be in charge of punishing people for bragging about good luck hears about her bad luck, too. *"¡Muchas cosas desagradables!"* Many unpleasant things!

Juanita knows she should be helping Tía Lola ward off bad luck, but she's too curious. "I thought you were really happy here, Tía Lola. Like what bad things have happened?"

Her aunt's forehead furrows as she tries desperately to think of something to complain about. *"Bueno,* well . . . it has been cold for a long time." Just then, a burst of sunlight splashes through the window, flooding the bus with summery warmth. Tía Lola sighs, giving up. There is no denying it. She has had a very lucky life lately.

From the back of the bus comes the sound of Miguel's voice reporting on some play by the Knicks at the Madison Square Garden game.

"*¡Ya, ya!*" Tía Lola cries out. "I know what very unlucky thing has been happening: *el inglés!* Learning English is too hard. In the *restaurante,* the eggplant has no egg. The hamburger no ham. We serve dessert, but no one can desert the table to go to a desert because there are none in Vermont. More than one goose is 'geese,' but more than one moose is not 'meese.' No, no, no! *Es muy difícil.* It's too hard to learn. *¡Me voy a volver loca aprendiendo inglés!*"

Is Tía Lola really going to go crazy learning English, or is she just saying so to ward off bad luck for bragging about her good luck? Just when Juanita is starting to worry about her aunt, Tía Lola winks. Her beauty mark, usually painted on the right side of her upper lip, dots her left cheek today. It makes Juanita smile to see it there. If Tía Lola were not in her life, Juanita would be a very unhappy, very unlucky girl, that's for sure. Juanita squeezes her eyes shut and concentrates real hard. It's her *costumbre*—instead of doing Tía Lola's sign of the cross— to close her eyes and make a wish when she really needs good luck.

● ● ●

That night, bad luck moves in like yet another cold front. Mami goes through the mail and finds a letter from the

United States Department of Immigration saying that the visitor's visa of María Dolores Milagros Santos is about to expire. She must report to her local immigration office and be prepared to leave the country immediately. Mami's face gets as pale as a brown person's face can get.

"¿Qué pasa, Mami?" Juanita wants to know what's wrong. Already her heart is beating hard, remembering the bad-luck conversation this morning on the bus.

But Mami is too preoccupied to explain. "What do they mean, she has to leave immediately? But we applied . . . The lawyer said . . . How can they separate a family this way?"

"Mami, who are you talking about?" Juanita asks desperately. It's horrible when you see your parents in a panic but you don't know what is upsetting them!

"María Dolores Milagros Santos," Mami explains unhelpfully. Then she must realize Juanita and Miguel have no idea who this person is. "Your *tía* Lola. That's her real name."

No wonder Tía Lola is having bad luck, with a name like that! After all, *dolores* is the word for "sufferings" in Spanish. Imagine being named Sufferings! Of course, *milagros* means "miracles," so maybe that cancels out the suffering? Juanita certainly hopes so.

"No hay que ahogarse en un vaso de agua," Tía Lola counsels calmly. Let's not drown in a glass of water. This is what she always says when anyone gets too worked up about a small matter.

96

But if Tía Lola has to leave them, that is a very big deal. "She's like our grandmother," Juanita says weepily.

"Perhaps I can go and come back. You know, like I did last Christmas."

Mami shakes her head. "Remember what the lawyer told us? The visa was for sixteen months, no extensions. But he was going to apply for your residency card so you could stay. He said it shouldn't be a problem when I explained you were like my mother. After we paid him all that money . . ." Mami's voice trails away. She sinks down in her chair, defeated.

Miguel has been sitting by, racking his brains about how to help his family. He has told the mugging story so many times that he has come to think of himself as a superhero. In fact, he has been awaiting the opportunity to truly rescue somebody. Here it is. But what to do? He hasn't a clue.

The mugging story, of course, makes him think of Carmen. And then it dawns on him. "Why don't we call Carmen? She's a lawyer." The minute Miguel makes his suggestion, he worries that his *mami* will be upset. But instead of annoyance, a wave of relief sweeps over his mother's face.

"She isn't actually an immigration lawyer, but still . . ." Mami is thinking out loud. "She does work in a big firm. She's bound to know someone who knows about visas. Maybe she can help us."

Mami calls Papi to get Carmen's number. Soon the

two women are having a long conversation. Juanita and Miguel and Tía Lola sit around the table, watching Mami's every expression. Before Mami hangs up, Carmen promises to call back after she speaks to some of her colleagues at work. Maybe something will work out.

Please, please! Juanita closes her eyes for the second time today and makes her wish: *Let Tía Lola stay with my family!*

●●●

Somehow the news spreads through town and at school. Tía Lola might have to leave the country.

"But she can't!" Mrs. Stevens folds her arms and plants herself at the entrance to her school. She will not let anyone take her best volunteer away. "Who will teach the children Spanish? Who will organize *carnaval* parties and treasure hunts and paint murals to liven up the halls?"

"Who will run Spanish night?" Rudy says, shaking his head when he hears the news. "Who's going to teach us to dance the merengue and cook *flan* and that great rice-and-beans dish *arroz con habichoolas*?"

"*Arroz con habichuelas,*" Tía Lola corrects him, but without her usual lively smile. Being asked to leave the country has made her feel like a guest who has overstayed her welcome.

"Who will make piñatas for me to sell?" Stargazer sighs. "And help me paint the sale signs for the store?"

Woody, Rudy's son, sums up the whole town's

feelings: "Tía Lola can't leave. She's the best thing that's happened to this town since . . ."

"Since the pilgrims came!" Dawn says, and that's saying a lot, seeing as her ancestors came over on the *Mayflower*.

"Well, let's not get carried away!" Colonel Charlebois, who is having his daily meal at Amigos Café, says in his cranky voice. But in fact, what he's cranky about is this unwelcome news. "It certainly would be a sad state of affairs if Tía Lola left. One that I don't think any of us could bear!" He clears his throat again and again. Usually a man with a hearty appetite, he barely touches his *huevos rancheros,* although they're just the way he likes them tonight.

●●●

A few days later, Carmen calls Mami back. There are several options that would let Tía Lola stay in the USA. In order to arrive at a decision, Mami calls an informal town meeting over at Amigos Café for that Wednesday night.

The whole town shows up! The restaurant can't fit such a large crowd, so the gathering is moved across the street to the library's large meeting room.

Mami reads out all the possibilities Carmen's lawyer friend suggested. Among the options is applying for an "extraordinary ability" visa, awarded to someone with an exceptional skill the country can't do without. At the mention of this special visa, the whole town breaks into applause. "That's it!" people call out. "Go for it! We can't lose Tía Lola. She has the extraordinary ability to bring us all together!"

But Tía Lola still has to report to the immigration office on Friday to plead her case before a judge. Since Friday is an in-service day at school and there won't be any classes, Mrs. Stevens volunteers to accompany Tía Lola and speak up on her behalf. After all, this is part of her in-service, keeping this treasure in her school.

"I'm coming along, too," Mrs. Prouty says. "Without Tía Lola, I don't know what we'd do."

"Make that three of us!" Mr. Bicknell is always one to take up a cause if he believes it is fair and just.

Soon every teacher at Bridgeport has signed on, and that gets the students started. A group of sixth graders convince several parents to drive them up to the hearing. It'll be like a field trip: watching how the United States of America works. Before you know it, kids from every grade are clamoring to go. Of course, Rudy is shutting down his restaurant to head up there, and Woody volunteers his own van, and Colonel Charlebois has room in his car for three more—five if two are skinny, which could only be if they haven't discovered Amigos Café's fine cuisine, which is what Colonel Charlebois calls good cooking.

By the end of the evening, most of the town's inhabitants are planning to head up to the immigration office on Friday morning.

Juanita has been sitting in the front row, worrying and wondering what will happen. Mami has told her and Miguel privately—so as to prepare them—that Carmen did say the chances are that Tía Lola will not be able to stay right away. Every foreigner has to take a turn, with preference given to the immediate family of American citizens: sons and daughters, parents and grandparents. That means that although Tía Lola actually raised Mami, still, on paper, she only counts as an aunt. She will have to go to the back of the line.

But Juanita can't even imagine a life without Tía Lola anymore. It's like Mami keeps saying: How can the United States of America do that to her family? They might as well deport Juanita, too, even though she'd have to leave her mother and father and brother as well as her own country behind.

Beside her, Tía Lola has been sitting quietly all evening, occasionally dabbing at her eyes with one of the handkerchiefs that Carmen gave her, for happy tears. But Juanita is pretty sure Tía Lola's tears aren't happy. How can they be when she is being asked to leave a country where all she has done is spread love and happiness?

As the meeting is starting to break up, Tía Lola stands and asks if Mami will translate a few words.

When Mami announces that Tía Lola has something to say, the noisy, fired-up crowd sits down obediently. You can hear a pin drop, as well as *un alfiler*.

"I want to thank all of you," Tía Lola begins in a voice full of emotion, "for how you have welcomed me to your wonderful country. Whether or not I get to stay, I will always remain here, because you have let me into your hearts. And you will never be far from me, because I will take each and every one of you in *mi corazón* and in my memories." Tía Lola will take the whole town in her heart back to the Dominican Republic.

Mami grows teary-eyed as she translates. From her chair in the front row, Juanita herself is seeing a double Tía Lola and Mami through the tears in her eyes. Meanwhile, Miguel is ready to bolt out of his chair and protect Tía Lola if the guards come to take her away, just like Carmen protected him from Rafi in the subway.

Throughout the room, people are blowing their noses and coughing away their sadness. Tía Lola's words have a goodbye ring to them. But then her tone changes. "One last thing," she says, flashing her lively grin. "Before I leave, I promise that with your help, I'm going to put up a good fight to stay!"

Once again, the room breaks out clapping and cheering, except this time the response is louder, fiercer, and seems to go on forever. Even Melrose, the town clerk, has to admit that he has never seen anything like this. "Maybe Tía Lola should run for governor or something."

"Nunca es tarde cuando la dicha es buena," Tía Lola concludes before she sits back down.

Mami struggles to translate the saying. "It's never too

102

late when you're in luck. Or something like that. Anyhow, thanks, everyone, for helping us out!"

Instead of clapping and stomping her feet, Juanita closes her eyes. *Please, please, please,* let Tía Lola stay, she wishes with all her might. She tries it in Spanish for double strength: *¡Por favor, por favor, por favor, que tía Lola se pueda quedar!* And then Juanita can't help herself. She touches her forehead, her heart, her two shoulders, then kisses her thumb, sealing the biggest wish she can ever remember making in her life so far.

lesson nine

En la unión está la fuerza
In unity there's strength

Along with everyone else in the county, Miguel wakes up on Friday morning with a hopeful, fearful feeling. By the end of the day, Tía Lola's fate will be decided. Mami has warned him and Juanita not to get their hopes up too high. But how can they help it when the day dawns so sunny and warm and bright?

After breakfast, Tía Lola appears at the door with a little suitcase. Miguel's heart feels like a pebble dropped in a well, leaving an empty hole in his chest. "What are you doing with that *maleta*?" he asks, as if he can't guess.

"Por si acaso," Tía Lola says brightly. Just in case. "But

notice how small it is, Miguel. If I go away, I won't be gone long."

Mami makes light of the suitcase as well. "It's the 'raincoat lucky charm.' If you wear your raincoat, it won't rain. If Tía Lola takes her suitcase, she won't be sent away."

Miguel groans. He can remember any number of times his *mami* has made him wear a rain slicker and it still has rained.

"Now, now, Miguel Ángel Guzmán," Mami reminds him. "You'll make your *tía* Lola nervous if *you* get too nervous. And remember, she has to charm the socks off the immigration judge. We have to present a united front. As Tía Lola likes to say—"

"En la unión está la fuerza." Tía Lola quotes her own saying: In unity there's strength. It sounds like something from the Declaration of Independence. That should charm the socks off an immigration judge!

"Hey, Tía Lola, why don't you just quote your wise sayings to the judge?" Miguel says, half in jest. "That'll show him why we can't let you go."

Mami drops down on the bench in the mudroom. It's as if she has just had a suspicion confirmed. "Now I know it's a fact: I have a genius son! That is a brilliant idea!"

Miguel loves a compliment as much as the next person, but Mami can go overboard. And when you get praised too much, it's like you're an animal paralyzed by headlights on the road: there's no wiggle room to make a mistake or even improve at something you're already good at.

"Tía Lola, we'll prove to the judge that you're our town oracle!" Mami claps her hands.

"What's that?" Juanita asks. She wonders if an oracle is anything like a barnacle, a word she learned just last week in school when they were studying beach flora and fauna. But Tía Lola doesn't remind Juanita in the least of those little shellfish that attach themselves to cliffs and the sides of ships.

"An oracle is a person or place or even a book full of wise knowledge." Mami launches into an explanation about the Delphic Oracle in Greece; how in olden times in China, people consulted this oracular book called the *I Ching*. . . .

Miguel is half listening, half daydreaming. After so many ho-hum weeks, it's going to be an exciting day! Papi couldn't miss any more work, but Carmen is actually flying up with an immigration lawyer from her firm who has agreed to represent Tía Lola. They will all meet up at the immigration office.

At first, Mami hesitated when Carmen made her offer. "I don't know that we can afford that, Carmen. That last lawyer wiped us out."

"Oh, don't worry about it. There's no charge," Carmen had assured her.

But after hanging up, Mami was thoughtful. "I have a feeling that maybe Carmen is paying for this herself."

"She is a true friend," Tía Lola acknowledged, a hand on her heart. *"Amiga en la adversidad es amiga de verdad."* A friend in adversity is a true friend.

If Tía Lola can keep saying her sayings, surely she will get that special visa. Miguel doesn't feel like he is cheating his country in any way. Tía Lola does have so many extraordinary abilities. Look at all she has done for their little town. Free Spanish lessons, good food, and that special magic of hers that brings everyone together. Plus her sayings *are* wise. Miguel suddenly feels hopeful. It can't be every day that the Department of Immigration gets an application for a special visa from an oracle—with a genius for a nephew, at that!

●●●

By the time Miguel, Juanita, Tía Lola, and Mami arrive, a crowd has gathered in front of the no-nonsense, box-like brick building. DEPARTMENT OF HOMELAND SECURITY, a large sign announces. Several police cars are parked directly in front of the building, and the pathway to the door is blocked by sawhorse barricades. The officers look baffled as to why such a multitude has descended on their sleepy little town on a sunny April morning.

The minute Tía Lola appears, the crowd cheers. The three policemen are suddenly at attention, ready to protect the building against any attack. But coming toward them is a nice-looking young woman in an elegant black pantsuit, accompanied by a boy and a girl dressed up real nice as well. Behind them—must be the grandmother— is a perky, older lady with a jaunty purple flower in her hair and a bright yellow scarf draped over her coat. Only thing a little different about the family is their brown skin and their super-courteous manners. They stop to explain who they are, apologizing for any disturbance. So this is the family everyone has been expecting.

"Your lawyers just went in," one of the officers explains. "They're waiting for you inside."

"Thank you, sir," Mami says, eyeing Miguel and Juanita, who chime in, "Thank you, sir, thank you." On the ride up, Mami has coached them, using Tía Lola's saying about catching flies with a drop of honey, not a quart of vinegar.

"Muchas gracias," Tía Lola echoes in Spanish, adding, *"El amor lo vence todo."* It's one of her sayings: Love conquers all.

"Not yet, Tía Lola," Miguel whispers. She should save her sayings for later. This officer is not the person Tía Lola has to impress.

But Tía Lola's smile is so radiant, the gruff-looking man smiles back. "Watch your step," he cautions, and opens the door for her!

Inside, Carmen is so happy to see them, she gives them all hugs, even though she and Mami usually just shake hands. When they are done with their greetings, a tall brown-skinned man steps forward. His hair is black and disheveled, his glasses small and round. He looks more like an absentminded professor than a sharp New York City lawyer. *"Ay, perdóname,"* Carmen apologizes. She introduces her lawyer friend, whose specialty is immigration law: Víctor Espada. That *is* a lucky omen, Miguel can't help thinking: a lawyer whose name means "victory sword."

"Hola, mucho gusto," he greets them in perfect Spanish. It turns out that Víctor's ancestors came from Mexico a long time ago. "Actually, they didn't come *here* as much as the United States came to *them* in 1848." Miguel remembers learning about the Mexican-American War in history class, how a whole chunk of the Southwest was handed over by Mexico when the United States won the war.

After the introductions, Mami explains about the oracle idea her brilliant son came up with. "Sounds like a plan," Víctor says, giving Miguel a man-to-man nod. It's enough of a compliment without being all gushy, which Miguel appreciates.

"What do you say we bring in a few of the town's prominent citizens to speak up for Tía Lola?" Víctor looks over at Miguel like they are planning this case together. That is how Mrs. Stevens and Rudy and Colonel Charlebois, dressed in his old army uniform, are allowed inside the building.

Once their party is all assembled, the switchboard person calls for a Homeland Security officer to come escort them to the hearing room, where Judge Reginald Laliberte is waiting for them.

"Reginald Laliberte?" Colonel Charlebois recognizes the name. "Why, I shipped out to Korea with his father. Got shot down. Left the family fatherless. Mother died soon thereafter. Heard the six kids were farmed out to relatives, a couple to a home. Last I heard, some did well, some ended up behind bars. I guess we're about to see one of the ones who did okay. Reggie's son—who would have thought!"

Miguel isn't sure if this is good news or bad news. Sounds like this judge has had a tough life, and sometimes that can make a person be tough on everyone else. But it's too late to request an alternate.

They file down the hall quietly, overtaken by the somber air of the place. The walls are bare, except for a few posters with warnings (no smoking, no firearms, no photographs)—nothing cheerful like kittens playing with balls of yarn or photographs of pretty scenes in Vermont. Only Tía Lola seems relaxed, smiling eagerly, as if she's about to enter a party rather than a room where her fate will soon be decided.

"Aren't you nervous, Tía Lola?" Miguel whispers just before they go in.

"A mal tiempo, buena cara," she replies, flashing him an extra bright smile. In bad times, put on a good face. And that's exactly what she does when she stands before the judge, who sits behind a big desk on a raised platform. He is an older man, gray-haired but with eyebrows that have not aged: they are an astonishing jet-black. This gives him a stern look, as if he is permanently scowling.

"Good morning," he says, not unkindly. "Looks like spring has finally arrived." Miguel knows the gray-haired man is talking about the sunny day outside the window. But he can't help thinking that perhaps the judge is also paying a compliment to Tía Lola's colorful flowered dress, now in full display as she removes her coat.

"Una golondrina no hace el verano," Tía Lola reminds him. "We'll have to wait and see if spring is here!"

Víctor translates the saying.

"Very wisely put," the judge says, making a note on his pad. "One swallow does not make a summer," he murmurs, chuckling to himself.

"It doesn't make a summer, but it's a start," Tía Lola adds, winking at the judge when he looks up from his notepad.

●●●

Mami is the first witness. The judge wants to know the whole story of why Tía Lola came up from the Dominican Republic. As Mami talks, he listens, head bowed, so he looks like he's praying. Every once in a while, he glances up, as if verifying with a probing glance the truth of some remark.

Mami begins by explaining how Tía Lola took care of her as a little girl after her *mami* and *papi* died. (The judge looks up. Maybe he's thinking about the deaths of his own parents?) How Mami got the opportunity to come to the States to study; how she met her husband, also an

111

immigrant; how they married, had two kids, separated, divorced. (Mami hurries through this part.) How she took a job in Vermont. How she needed another family member in the household to help with her kids when they came home from school. How Tía Lola came to visit and then decided to stay. How her visa was for sixteen months and is now about to expire. How they went to a lawyer and paid him a lot of money to help get Tía Lola a residency card so she could stay with the family, but he must not have done anything because Tía Lola just got a notice that she has to leave.

"I know she's not technically my mother or the kids' grandmother, but she really is to us." Mami's voice starts to quiver. "Please, Judge, sir, don't tear my family apart."

Miguel hopes with all his might that his *mami* won't cry. For one thing, that'll get Juanita started; then Carmen, who cries at the drop of a hat; and soon, Tía Lola will be bawling. This tough judge might decide this country doesn't need more crybabies.

"Your aunt, or I should say your mother, certainly sounds like a very important member of your family," the judge concedes to Mami. "And from the size of the crowd out there"—he nods toward the window—"she must also be a beloved member of your community."

"I can attest to that," Colonel Charlebois says, coming forward, leaning on his cane. "This individual is one of the best things that has ever happened to our town. And I've been around for a long time. Even served with your father!"

The judge glances up at the old man in a worn army uniform. For a moment he looks as if he is seeing a ghost from the past.

"Your father was a true hero," Colonel Charlebois adds, drawing himself up as straight as he's ever going to get and giving the gray-haired man a firm salute.

Slowly, the judge lifts one hand and salutes back.

● ● ●

After a brief recess, Tía Lola is next. The judge begins by asking her what she thinks of all this praise.

"They make me sound like a big hero, but I'm not," Tía Lola explains in Spanish. Miguel shakes his head, contradicting his aunt. Tía Lola is supposed to be convincing the judge that she is extraordinary, not telling him she's not! "But better than being an important person is being important to the people you love. *Mejor ser cabeza de ratón que rabo de león.*"

The judge laughs when Víctor translates Tía Lola's saying. "Better to be the head of a rat than the tail of a lion," he murmurs to himself as he writes down the saying in his pad.

One by one, the witnesses get up and attest to the worth of Tía Lola. Finally, when all the adults have had their say, the judge turns to Juanita and Miguel. "I guess the only two people I haven't heard from in this room are you two. Will you come forward and introduce yourselves?"

113

Juanita jumps right up and approaches the bench. "My name is Juana Inés Guzmán, but everyone—except Carmen—calls me Juanita," she rattles off easily. Before the judge can even ask her a question, Juanita has launched into how Tía Lola is like her combination grandmother, favorite aunt, and best friend. If she is forced to leave the United States, Juanita wants permission to go with her.

"Well, that would be a great loss to our country," the judge says, looking genuinely concerned about losing Juanita to the Dominican Republic. "I hope you're not going to abandon ship as well," he says, craning his neck in order to look behind Juanita to where Miguel is still sitting. For some reason, Miguel has not been able to move. His legs might as well be two blocks of concrete. He feels almost as scared as he did when Rafi slammed him against the wall in the subway.

"Come forward, young man," the judge urges him again. "Nothing to be afraid of."

"He's not afraid!" Tía Lola defends her nephew. "He just knows silence is precious. *En boca cerrada no entran moscas.*" No flies can enter a closed mouth.

The judge roars with laughter. "You are a lively lady, all right!"

"You should see her on Wednesday nights," Rudy speaks up. He explains about the wonderful community dinners, the menu in Spanish, the dance lessons. "Amigos Café—come down and check it out."

"Sounds like this individual *is* pretty extraordinary!

But I would like to hear from the young man. You know, our American boys and girls are our national treasure. And a word from them is worth any dozen testimonies from us old fogies."

Given that summons, how can Miguel not come forward? Suddenly, his legs are as light as if he were that Greek god Mercury, with wings on his ankles and on his cap. He walks to the platform and looks up at the gray-haired man with stern eyebrows but surprisingly kind eyes.

"What have you got to say to add to this chorus of praise for Ms. Lola?"

And so Miguel tells him. How heartbroken he was when his parents separated. How he feels very lucky because slowly his family is re-forming in new ways. "She's actually going to be my stepmother," Miguel says, pointing to Carmen, who bows her head to hide her grateful tears. Then, pointing to Mami, he adds, "My *mami* is great at her job, but sometimes she has to work real late. Tía Lola is the only family we have in Vermont to help take care of us." Actually, Tía Lola has held all the broken pieces of their family together during tough times. But Miguel doesn't want to get too mushy in front of this crowd.

As Miguel speaks, the judge gazes intently at him, as if something in this boy reminds him of his younger self. "At first, I wasn't sure about Tía Lola joining our family, because she was kind of different and I was afraid kids would make fun of us. But then Tía Lola came to our school and everybody fell in love with her."

115

"She's the best thing that has happened to Bridge-port Elementary School," Mrs. Stevens adds.

"She's like our barnacle," Juanita says, getting her two new words confused. But it works: Tía Lola is like an or-acle, but she's also like a barnacle, attached to everyone, part of the flora and the fauna of their town.

"And if you don't believe me, you can ask all the kids out there," Miguel concludes. "They'll all tell you the same thing."

The judge lays down his pen. He takes a deep breath, as if he wants to bring up his verdict from deep inside him. "I don't have it in me to break a whole community's heart. Or yours," he adds, nodding at Juanita and Miguel. "We'll find a way for your *tía* Lola to stay," he promises. "Meanwhile, I'm going to grant her an extension of three more months so her lawyers can get her residency papers in order." He nods at Carmen and Víctor.

From deep inside Miguel comes a shout of joy. Juanita's cry follows. Soon their whole group is laughing and high-fiving and hugging each other. Tía Lola hurries to the window and waves her yellow scarf, a victory sign for the cheering crowd.

"Order in the courtroom!" The judge is now stand-ing at the podium, gavel in hand, as if he means to bang it on their heads to quiet them down. The room goes deathly still. "Before you take off," he says, pausing for effect, "what was the name of that restaurant?"

❋❋❋

As they walk down the hall, Tía Lola slips her arm around Miguel. "I think your words made all the difference," she whispers. "I saw that judge's face change as you spoke. You probably reminded him of himself, and his heart was moved. Thank you, Miguel. You are my hero."

And you are mine, Miguel thinks, but that's just too corny to say out loud in front of all these people. Instead, Miguel quotes another favorite saying of Tía Lola's: *"De tal palo, tal astilla."* The wood is where the splinter comes from. Like father, like son. Like grandmother, like grandson. In other words, if he's a hero, he got it from his aunt!

lesson ten

Corazón contento es gran talento
Being happy is a great talent

On the third Saturday in June, just before school lets out, Bridgeport Elementary will have its end-of-the-year picnic.

Usually only staff, teachers, and students and their parents attend, but this year the whole town is invited. There is something special to celebrate: Tía Lola is on her way to becoming a permanent resident of the United States of America! She will be able to stay for as long as she wants.

And something else to celebrate: the town has learned so much Spanish that half the time, instead of calling out "Hi!" people greet each other on the street with *"¡Hola!"*

"¿Cómo estás?" they'll ask, instead of "How are you?" *"Muy, muy bien."* Everyone seems to be doing very, very well. *"¡Qué buena noticia lo de Tía Lola!"* And what good news about Tía Lola!

"Did you hear that the judge is coming to the picnic?" *"¿Es verdad?"* Could it really be true?!

"¡Sí, señor!" Yes, sir!

Papi and Carmen are also coming, and they're bringing Abuelito and Abuelita with them. Abuelita has sufficiently recovered from her winter *quebrantos* to make the trip. Whatever is left of her ailments will be cured by seeing *both* her grandchildren.

Coming with them, curiously eager to get back to Vermont, will be Tía Lola's lawyer, Víctor Espada. Víctor has been calling daily with news about the progress of Tía Lola's application, news that isn't really new, since he calls every night with the same information. Tía Lola talks briefly, and then she puts Mami on so Víctor can tell her the news as well. For the next hour, Víctor and Mami talk and talk. They also seem to laugh a whole lot.

The only sad part of the happy ending of the school year is that Ofie and her sisters won't be able to come to the picnic. Unlike Tía Lola, their parents didn't come with visas, and now the whole family is being deported back to Mexico.

Mrs. Stevens calls an assembly to make the announcement. "I'm sorry," she says, as if it were her fault. "The girls are temporarily staying with a friend of the family while their parents' deportation is being processed. We are in touch with them. They are all well, I promise." Mrs. Stevens then reads a letter written by the girls in which they thank the school, the principal, the teachers and staff, the students, and most of all, Tía Lola. "They send many hugs and hearts and kisses," Mrs. Stevens closes. She holds up the letter. Several big red hearts are visible at the bottom. "I'll post the letter on the entrance bulletin board so you can all read it."

Before dismissing the assembly, Mrs. Stevens tries to raise the school's flagging spirits by bringing up what they're all now calling Tía Lola's picnic. "It'd be wonderful if we came up with some surprise for Tía Lola. So be thinking about some ideas."

But in spite of the excitement about the picnic, a gloomy cloud hangs over the school for the rest of the day. Especially in Juanita's classroom, where Ofie's empty desk is a constant reminder. Once again, Juanita has trouble concentrating on her schoolwork. But it's not because she's daydreaming about some made-up story. This time it's real life that is troubling and absorbing.

"When I grow up," Juanita announces that night at dinner, "I'm going to be a lawyer."

Mami is all smiles. "Just like Víctor, eh?"

"Carmen, too," Miguel reminds her.

"But why do you want to be an *abogada*?" Tía Lola questions.

"So I can help people like Ofie and her family stay here," Juanita replies.

"A genius for a son and an angel for a daughter." Mami sighs. "How lucky can I get!"

Tía Lola quickly makes her sign of the cross. "Just to be sure," she explains when Mami looks over at her. After all, Mami is bragging about her children. *"Más vale prevenir que lamentar."*

"I guess it *is* better to be safe than sorry." Mami checks her watch and begins clearing the plates.

As he is helping dry the dishes, Miguel asks, "Mami, is it my imagination, or do people who speak Spanish really love sayings?"

Mami looks thoughtful. "I think we just notice them more when they come in a new language. I mean, there are hundreds of good sayings in English. We use them all the time, automatically." Mami pauses, and Miguel can tell she is trying to come up with some examples.

Just then the phone rings. In a moment, Tía Lola is calling out, "Linda!"

Mami dries her hands hurriedly. Then, recalling that she still hasn't come up with some sayings in English, she apologizes. "I'm drawing a total blank. But you know what? I'll ask Víctor. He's really good at stuff like that."

In fact, Mami and Víctor come up with a whole list of sayings. Talking to him seems to loosen up Mami's creative juices. After she hangs up, she even thinks up a dozen more on her own. Before saying good night to Miguel, Mami hands him several pages filled with proverbs and sayings.

That's why the next day, when Mrs. Stevens visits his classroom to collect proposals for Tía Lola's surprise, Miguel raises his hand. The one thing Tía Lola really wants is to learn English. The three things Tía Lola really, really loves are making piñatas, teaching at Bridgeport, and using sayings. Miguel has put all these things together and come up with what his *mami* would call another one of his brilliant ideas.

❋❋❋

Hanging from the big sugar maple in the playground is Miguel's brilliant idea for a surprise for Tía Lola: a piñata that is an exact replica of Bridgeport Elementary. When Tía Lola arrives at the picnic, she lets out a cry. Now she knows why she was forbidden to enter the art room for the last week or so.

But she has her own amazing surprise, covered in a bedsheet. When she unveils it, everyone gasps. No way! It also is a schoolhouse piñata, although not exactly a replica of Bridgeport. This building is painted purple, and instead of BRIDGEPORT ELEMENTARY SCHOOL, the turquoise sign above the door reads LA ESCUELITA BRIDGEPORT. An extreme makeover of their little school, in color and in *español*!

"Great minds think alike," Mami and Víctor say at the same time. Then they both burst out laughing, and for a few minutes, it looks like they might not be able to stop.

"Order in the picnic!" the judge declares, which just makes everyone else join in the laughter.

Abuelito and Abuelita sit on folding chairs near the food table, which is crammed with dishes Abuelita brought up from New York City. It's as if she feared starvation in Vermont. By the end of the afternoon, she might well assume that all Vermonters are starving: there won't be a crumb left to scrape into a take-home container.

Looking out at the gathering, Miguel can't believe how happy he feels. Before him are most of the special people in his life. What's more, the golden days of summer stretch ahead, with game after game of baseball in the field behind his house. And the best news of all is that Tía Lola will get to stay. Their family won't be torn apart again.

Juanita is also feeling lucky, especially when she thinks of Ofie. Someday, if she doesn't become a lawyer, she wants to write a book about a little Mexican girl who comes to a farm in Vermont and gets to stay. Just thinking about that ending makes her heart flood with happiness.

"Okay, it's time," Mrs. Stevens announces. "How shall we do this? Shall we begin with our piñata or Tía Lola's?"

It's no use taking a vote. Some people call out, "Tía Lola's!" including Tía Lola, and others shout, "Ours!"

"Why don't you decide?" Mrs. Stevens asks the judge. After all, he is the highest-ranking official at the gathering.

"Oh, no!" Judge Reginald shakes his head. "I don't want to decide a single thing today, except what I'm going to eat next." He heads toward the food table, where Abuelita is already on her feet, ready to dish him out some more of her *puerco asado*. "This has got to be the best roast pork I've ever tasted," the judge declares. "And I'm willing to swear on a stack of Bibles," he tells Abuelita, who already believes him, given the proof of a third serving.

"Okay," Mrs. Stevens says, handing Tía Lola a broom. "You go first. After all, you are our guest of honor." There's no need to blindfold Tía Lola, as only she gets to swipe at the piñata the school made for her.

My oh my! Who would have thought a woman Tía Lola's age would be such a powerhouse? In a matter of three hits, the schoolhouse explodes.

Raining down are dozens upon dozens of folded-up pieces of paper. *"¿Qué será?"* Tía Lola picks a few up, intrigued. "Fortunes?"

Mrs. Stevens laughs. "No, no, Tía Lola. This was your nephew's idea. He said there were three things you really love: Piñatas, so we made you one. Teaching at Bridgeport, so we made your piñata our schoolhouse. And sayings, so each student has chosen a saying in English for you, with a short explanation. That way, you can learn more English. You have all summer to study them."

You'd think Tía Lola had just gotten a treasure chest full of gold! She goes down on her knees, picking up all the scattered pieces of paper and putting them in one of the shopping bags she brought for the food containers. *"Gracias, gracias, gracias,"* she keeps saying as she drops each one in.

Now it's Tía Lola's turn to present her piñata. First, she has some words she wants to say in English. "When I come to the United Estates, only I have three people in my *familia* here: my big niece, my little niece, my nephew. But now I have a big *familia* of friends. Thank you, all the students and teachers and Señora Stevens, for allowing me the *oportunidad* to learn how to teach at *la escuelita* Bridgeport."

Miguel and Juanita are amazed. Where did Tía Lola learn to make a whole speech in English? The mystery is solved when they catch Rudy giving Tía Lola the thumbs-up.

Tía Lola's purple schoolhouse piñata is hoisted up on the branch beside the shreds of her own surprise. To start things off, Mrs. Stevens is allowed one honorary whack. She misses by a yard and hits a branch so hard, a bird's nest comes tumbling down on her head! Everyone tries to keep a straight face. But all it takes is one stray giggle, and the picnickers explode with laughter.

The kindergarteners go next. But most of them are so small that they end up whacking the air. It's only when the blindfolds are tied to the third graders that the whacking gets serious. Too bad, Miguel thinks. At this rate, the fifth (soon to be sixth) graders will never get a turn.

Finally, Milton delivers the fateful blow. Down rain dozens upon dozens of folded-up notes. "What in the world is that?" Milton asks, sounding disappointed. Every other piñata he has ever hit was full of candy and party favors.

"No son fortunas tampoco," Tía Lola says, shaking her head. These are not fortunes either, but sayings in Spanish. Talk about great minds thinking alike! Each person should take one and learn it, so that the town will not only become bilingual, but doubly wise as well.

Meanwhile, so as not to disappoint the children, Tía Lola pulls out several shopping bags she has tucked under the food table. As if she were scattering birdseed, she flings handful after handful of candies and dollar-store trinkets. The children scramble to get their American treats and their Spanish sayings: one disappears immediately, the other one is for keeps.

● ● ●

On the drive home from the picnic, Mami and Tía Lola, Miguel and Juanita, reminisce about the picnic. What fun they all had! What's more, the fun isn't over.

Following behind them in a rented van are Papi and Carmen, Abuelita and Abuelito, and Víctor—all of whom will be staying at the big house tonight. "There's plenty of space!" Mami had offered generously. Every time Papi and Carmen have come in the past, they've had to stay at the less-than-friendly B&B down the road.

Tía Lola approves of Mami's change of heart: *"Amor con amor se paga."* Love is repaid with love. Look at all that Carmen has done for their family.

"Víctor, too," Mami adds.

Speaking of Víctor, he has already made plans to

come back later this summer with his three kids to look around. It turns out that he is thinking of relocating to Vermont. This seems a wonderful place for a widowed father to raise a family.

"Wasn't that funny about the two piñatas?" Mami asks, looking in the rearview mirror to make sure her guests are following.

"My favorite was the nest," Juanita says, giggling all over again. Mrs. Stevens looked so silly with it sitting on her head.

"It's a good thing it was empty." Mami laughs. "I don't think she would have appreciated an egg shampoo." They all laugh.

"That judge has the appetite of a giant," Tía Lola remarks after the laughter dies down.

"Maybe he didn't get much to eat as a kid." Miguel reminds them of the story they heard from Colonel Charlebois about the judge's tough childhood.

"Good point, Miguel." Mami looks in the mirror, glowing with pride at her thoughtful son. "Wow, Tía Lola! I think all your sayings have actually made my children wiser."

"And I myself will grow wiser, with all my new sayings in English." Tía Lola pats the big plastic bag crammed into the front seat beside her.

"You sure we can't put that in back?" Mami offers again. But Tía Lola refuses to lose sight of her treasure.

"El ojo del amo engorda el caballo," Tía Lola explains. The eye of the owner fattens the horse.

"That's gross, Tía Lola!" Juanita wrinkles her nose. It sounds totally yucky to be feeding a horse your eyeballs! Juanita rolls down her window, thinking she might get carsick.

"No, no," Tía Lola says, laughing. "The saying means that when you keep an eye on things, they prosper." She pats the bag again, as if it were a horse.

Maybe because they are talking about sayings, Tía Lola asks if everyone has had a chance to look at their sayings from her piñata.

Juanita isn't sure where she put hers. For a few frantic moments, it looks like they might have to pull over and look inside her backpack in the trunk. But finally, she finds it tucked in her own pocket. She unfolds it sheepishly.

"So what does it say?" Miguel asks. After so much fuss, it'd better be good.

"I don't know how to read Spanish." Juanita tries handing the piece of paper to Tía Lola.

"Of course you do," Tía Lola encourages her. "Just remember, in Spanish you sound out every syllable."

"*Camarón que se duerme*— Wait a minute!" Juanita cries out, as if she has won the lottery. "I already know this saying." After her initial delight at the serendipity, Juanita feels cheated. "I wanted to learn a new one."

"Maybe you still have a lot to learn from that saying, you think?" Mami suggests.

"I suppose." Juanita sighs. How does Mami find out these things? Ever since Ofie's departure, Juanita *has* had

128

trouble keeping her mind on her schoolwork. But it's almost summer. Even shrimp have to sleep sometimes! Next year she'll be in fourth grade, with tons more work. Her brain needs a vacation. "What about you, Mami?" Juanita comes forward in her seat. "Which one did you get?"

"Oh, let's see," Mami says airily, even though she checked her saying when she and Víctor reached for the same piece of paper. "Mine says, *El amor lo vence todo.*" Love conquers all. The very saying Tía Lola used to disarm the policeman up at the immigration office.

"Oh, that's such a good one, Mami." Juanita looks down disappointedly at her own saying. "Want to trade?" she asks, as if the sayings were baseball cards, not little pieces of paper.

"Sure," Mami says. "But first, let's hear what Miguel got. Maybe we can make this a three-way trade?"

Although Miguel had glanced at his saying at the picnic, he only vaguely remembers it. There was so much to do and eat and plan with his friends. Already, on Monday, his summer baseball team is coming over to try on the new uniforms Tía Lola has almost finished making. Afterward, they will go out in the field behind his house and play until it's too dark to see the bases.

Miguel reads his saying out loud now. *"Corazón contento es gran talento."* He doesn't even have to ask Tía Lola what it means. Being happy is a great talent.

"Good job!" Mami compliments Miguel's Spanish. "We're going to have to send you both down to the D.R.

so you can impress *la familia* with all the Spanish you've learned with Tía Lola."

"Oh, can we, Mami, can we?" Juanita has forgotten her lackluster saying. "Maybe we can all go again for Christmas? Maybe stop in Disney World on the way?"

"We shall see," Mami says in a voice that makes Miguel and Juanita feel hopeful.

And there's lots to be hopeful about: Colonel Charlebois has been talking to Mami about selling her the big house, with the monthly rent turning into installments. They won't have to come up with a big down payment. Maybe they won't have to move out after all.

"Why don't you reach in your bag and pick out one of yours, Tía Lola?" Mami suggests. "Let's see what your first English saying will be."

Tía Lola plunges a hand into her bag, swishes it around, and fishes out a neatly folded piece of paper. Carefully, she opens it up. Someone who could not come up with any more wise words for Tía Lola has drawn a big heart that says it all:

As Tía Lola says:

Todo lo bueno se acaba.

All good things must come to an end.

about tía lola's spanish

Tía Lola asked me to be sure and explain why, when she speaks only Spanish, you are reading her words in English.

This is the wonderful thing about stories and about the imagination. The impossible is possible. You can read a story about a magical aunt who doesn't know any English, and even though you don't speak a word of her language, you can totally understand what she is saying! It's why I love stories. They remember what we often forget and what Tía Lola reminds us: we are all one human family, even if we speak different languages and come from different countries.

But just in case you wondered, one of the ways we recognize that a word belongs in another language, *otra lengua,* is that we put it in italics. Sometimes when Tía Lola is speaking, I'll throw in a few *palabritas,* a few words, in Spanish. That's just to remind you that Tía Lola really and truly is speaking in Spanish, but because it's a story, you have the magical ability to hear her Spanish in English.

Whenever I use a Spanish word, I always give you its English translation or make sure you understand what the word means in that scene. I wouldn't want you to feel left out just because you are not yet bilingual! But my hope (and Tía Lola's) is that what you can do magically in a story—understand Spanish—will make you want to learn that magic in real life. Being bilingual is a wonderful way to connect ourselves with other people from other countries and understand what it means to live inside their words as well as their world.

Maybe you can find a Tía Lola in your neighborhood who can come to your school and teach everyone how to speak Spanish in *español.*

acknowledgments

Just as Tía Lola got a heart
from a secret admirer,
I am sending
each of you
who inspired me
or helped me write this book
a heart
full of thanks and *gracias*
from your not-so-secret admirer.

Weybridge
Elementary
School

Roberto
Veguez

Lyn Tavares

Susan
Bergholz

Naomi &
Violet

Erin Clarke

Bill Eichner

La Virgencita
de la
Altagracia